SYNOPSIS

When Kyle agreed to spend Christmas in England with family and friends, he didn't expect to meet Jon, the attractive and sexy cousin of his Dad's boyfriend's BFF. But that's exactly what happened.

A brief hook-up in England quickly turned into texts, calls, several video chats, and even a weekend together in New Mexico. Now, four months after their fateful meeting at Christmas, Jon is coming to visit Kyle in DC.

Kyle is very excited with the prospect of spending more time with Jon, but planning a fun—and romantic—time with Jon is only half the battle. Eventually Kyle will need to tell his Dad—who may have issues with the fact that Jon is thirteen years older than Kyle.

Sightseeing, a river cruise on the Potomac, figuring out how to broach the subject of an older man with Dad, and gathering support wherever he can, Kyle is doing everything he can to find love on the Potomac.

Love ON THE POTOMAC

NEW ADVENTURES IN LOVE · BOOK 3

RJ PETERSON

Love on the Potomac

New Adventures in Love, Book 3

Cover design & interior design and formatting by Ron Perry Graphic Design, rperrydesign.com

Cover content is for illustrative purposes only. Any person depicted on the cover is a model.Cover background photography by Ron Perry.

Editing by Lyrical Lines, lyricallines.net

Proofreading by Lisa Lakeland, LesCourt Author Services, lescourtauthorservices.com

Digital ISBN: 978-1-967317-04-2

Print ISBN: 978-1-967317-16-5

This is a work of fiction. Names, characters, places and incidents are either used fictitiously or are the product of the author's imagination. Any resemblance to actual persons, living or dead, business establishments, events, or locales is entirely coincidental.

Despite the assistance I received regarding Washington, DC and river cruising, any errors herein are mine and mine alone.

All products and/or brand names mentioned are registered trademarks of their respective holders/companies.

This novel contains mature sexual content. Reader discretion is advised.

This novel contains mature sexual content. Reader discretion is advised.

No Generative AI Training Use.

To Karen Bonnick

Author, friend, and mentor.
Your encouragement and guidance
help sustain me.

Thank you.

"Anything is possible when you have the right people there to support you."

- Misty Copeland

CONTENTS

A WORD ABOUT COVID

When I wrote my first book, Love On The Horizon, I wasn't expecting it to become a series, so I purposely set it in the fall of 2019, thus avoiding any reference to COVID-19. But then, something interesting happened...

As I continued to write that first book, I started to get ideas for additional stories in the same universe. Once I published Love On The Horizon, I started working on book two and made a decision. The New Adventures in Love series all happens in a parallel universe that is exactly like the world we live in—except there's no COVID pandemic.

We've all suffered enough in so many ways over the past two+ years, and I thought it might be nice for this series to be an escape from all that.

Acknowledgments

While I wrote the words in this book, many people helped make it all happen...

David, my husband, friend, and travel partner. Thanks for your support and for continuing to make me laugh for 42+ years. Here's to new adventures and many more laughs!

Dianne, Lisa, & Sammi, this book is so much better thanks to your guidance and input. I could not have done it without you.

David Warner, thank you for sharing your knowledge of Washington DC, especially Logan Circle and Judiciary Square and for suggesting an official job title for Kyle. The information you provided was invaluable.

Tricia & Dorothy, even though I invented my own version of a river cruise to fit in with the Potomac location, your insights into what an actual river cruise is like was so very helpful.

Sharon, K-lee, Melissa, Teresa, Tal, Hank, Gregory, Meredith, Annabella, Ann, and so many more – the word 'thanks' seems inadequate, but it's the only one I've got at the moment. Your belief in me and my writing helps me get through the day.

I love you all very much.

PROLOGUE

Friday, December 25 – Christmas night, Jon's room at the Mews, Stoney Hill, England

Jon exited the bathroom he shared with Kyle and crawled under the covers. After a moment, he heard Kyle; it sounded like he was brushing his teeth.

A couple of minutes later, his door to the bathroom opened, and Kyle stepped into the room, wearing only a pair of black boxer briefs.

"Merry Christmas, Jon," he said, joining him in bed. Jon reached for him, pulling him tightly to his chest and kissing him deeply.

They rolled together, stopping with Jon on top as he ground his thickening dick against Kyle's already hard member.

"God, you feel so good," he panted between kisses.

"You do too," Kyle replied, grabbing Jon's ass. "Can't believe I'm finally here with you."

"Well, it hasn't really been easy to spend much time together since someone's always around. Although I must admit, I didn't expect anything like this to happen when I agreed to come here with Samantha."

"I wasn't expecting this either, but I'm certainly not complaining." Kyle beamed at him.

Jon flipped Kyle around so that he was hovering over him and pressed their lips together again, probing Kyle's mouth and swiping at his tongue.

"God, I love how you taste." Jon sighed, peppering kisses down Kyle's chest.

He tongued Kyle's navel, and the coarse hair from his treasure trail tickled Jon's lips. He breathed against the material covering Kyle's rigid length, then slowly pulled down the front of his boxer briefs and tucked the waistband behind Kyle's balls. Inhaling Kyle's musky scent, Jon licked his cock from root to tip.

Kyle sighed as Jon continued his ministrations, sucking on the silky head and hollowing his cheeks as he took the sexy younger man deeper. Kyle pulled him back up and kissed him again, sliding his tongue along the seam of Jon's lips until Jon opened to him. Their tongues twisted together, and they moaned into each other's mouths.

After several minutes of hot and heavy kissing, Kyle groaned out, "Wanna taste your cock."

Jon settled onto his back as Kyle spun and straddled him so that his cock hovered over Jon's mouth, and he licked along the length of Jon's uncut dick.

Jon greedily took Kyle to the back of his throat while Kyle slipped his tongue between the head of Jon's cock and his foreskin.

"Mmm," he hummed, twirling his tongue around the crown and gathering up the precum there.

Jon gently sucked on Kyle's balls before moving back to his furry crease. He teased Kyle's pucker, then plunged his tongue into Kyle's hole.

"Ungh." Kyle panted. Pulling Jon's foreskin back, he licked around the head, then swallowed him down to the root. He continued moving up and down the shaft, gradually picking up speed.

Jon moved back to Kyle's cock, using his fingers to tease his rim as he nipped and bathed the head.

"I'm close," Kyle whispered, briefly pulling off Jon's cock. Then he went back to sucking as he pulled on Jon's balls.

Kyle's balls tightened, and he came, spilling his load down Jon's throat.

Jon hummed around the dick filling his mouth, doing his best to drink down every drop. Kyle redoubled his efforts, moving faster and faster until he was rewarded with Jon's release.

As their breathing slowed, Kyle moved around and up so that he and Jon were once again face-to-face. They kissed, tasting themselves on each other's lips.

"That was amazing," Jon said.

"Yeah, it was," Kyle agreed. "Is it okay if I stay?"

"Please," replied Jon. "I love to cuddle."

"I do too." Kyle turned over, becoming the little spoon. Jon hugged him tight against his chest as they drifted off to sleep.

CHAPTER 1

Tuesday, December 29 – Flight from London to Washington, DC

What the hell was I thinking? Kyle mused over his recent choices while he relaxed in his business-class seat—thanks, Dad—as the plane whisked its way across the Atlantic to Washington, DC. Of course, he thought, when I agreed to spend the holidays at the family home in Stoney Hill this year, I never expected to meet someone as fascinating as Jon.

Sure, I liked him as soon as I met him, and okay, I might have indulged in a bit of what I thought was harmless flirting, but I felt bad for him. He'd impulsively left Arizona and ended up on his cousin's doorstep in Massachusetts after a confrontation with his mom and what sounded like a rather messy breakup. Who knew that Samantha would have such a hot cousin, and that he'd end up spending Christmas with all of us? I thought if I paid a bit of attention to him, it might help get him out of his funk. And when Jon flirted back, it was pretty adorable. He seemed a bit shy, and something about that touched my heart. Then Christmas night happened— OMG, I never jump into bed with someone that quickly but no regrets from me. I know we just met and promised we'd keep in touch, but who knows if that will actually happen? Sure, I want to, but we live so far away from each other.

Ah well, it's true what they say: all good things must come to an end. Kyle deliberately cut off his musings. He pulled out his Kindle and read for a good part of the flight, trying to relax and not think about Jon. He didn't want to get his hopes up in case things didn't work out, and they didn't see each other again.

<hr>

ONCE HE WAS through baggage claim and customs, Kyle quickly texted his best friend, Neil, who'd agreed to pick him up at the airport. Neil had spent the holidays with his family in western Virginia and still had his rental car for one more day. That was so much better than riding the Metro while dragging his luggage back to his condo in Logan Circle.

Neil had texted Kyle a description of the SUV he was driving, so Kyle headed for the vehicle when he saw it pull up. After placing his bags in the back, he hopped into the passenger seat.

"So how was the family Christmas in England?" Neil asked as he pulled into traffic.

"It was great," Kyle answered with a smile. He buckled his seat belt, then turned toward his friend. "It felt good to spend time with everyone back in the family home. It had been too long since I'd last been there, so it was nice to finally be in England again. And oh my God, my dad got engaged! He and Rob went to Barcelona right after Christmas, and Dad popped the question. So there'll be a wedding later this year, I think."

Hey, that's great," Neil said. "They've been together about a year now, right?"

"Yeah, it was a year in October. While we were in England, they talked about moving in together, so this is the next step for them. I'm really happy for both of them; Rob's a great guy, and I can't remember my dad being happier than he is now."

"So, what about you, Kyle? Meet anyone interesting while you were there?" Neil queried.

Kyle felt his face flush. "Why would you ask that?"

"Aha! I knew it. You've done the deed since I last saw you. There's something different about you: your manner or how you're carrying yourself. I don't know exactly what it is, but I could tell something was different. Spill." He glared briefly at Kyle, then quickly turned it into a smile.

Kyle sighed. "I should have known better than to think I could keep something from you." Kyle thought back to the day he'd met Neil for the first time. They'd started with the financial investment company on the same day, five years ago, and being the new guys, began hanging out with each other. The more time they spent together—at lunch, for after-work drinks, etc. —the more they realized that had a lot in common. They were both unattached, interested in meeting the right man, and they lived in the same neighborhood. As a result, they soon became best friends. They'd actually tried dating once early in their friendship but soon realized they were much better as friends than lovers, and Kyle was grateful for Neil's support.

Kyle took a deep breath and continued. "Rob's best friend, Samantha, brought her cousin Jon with her. It was a last-minute thing. It seems he had a fight with his mom and showed up on Sam's doorstep unexpectedly. She called Rob and asked if she could bring him along, and of course, Rob said yes."

"And you two hooked up? How exactly did that happen?" Neil asked excitedly. Kyle couldn't help but smile at his friend's reaction. Neither one of them had had much of a love life recently.

"First of all, he's absolutely gorgeous. Remember the actor who played the werewolf on that show we binged? You know, the one with the vampires and that waitress that both the wolf and the vampire wanted? Jon kind of looks like the wolf guy."

"Seriously? Damn, man, when you finally land someone, you don't mess around, do you?"

"I don't think I said anything about 'landing someone,' Neil. We hung out together for about a week, and yeah, we hooked up Christmas night, but I'm not sure if it's gonna turn into anything long-term."

"But you just said that your dad is moving in with Rob, so if you go up to Massachusetts to visit, you'll get to see Jon again, right?" Neil asked.

"Well, that's part of the problem. Jon doesn't live in Massachusetts; he's from Phoenix. As in Arizona. When he had the fight with his mom, he jumped on a plane and flew to Massachusetts to be with Sam. And there's something else that I haven't told you yet," Kyle said.

"Hell, Phoenix is only a plane ride away. You can make this work if it's meant to be. And what haven't you told me yet?"

Kyle hesitated. Deep down, he knew Neil wouldn't care, but his dad was another story, so his feelings were a bit out of sort. "Um, he's a little older than me. Actually ... more than a little."

"Okay. Not that I think it matters, but how much?"

"Thirteen years."

"Dude! Way to go," Neil said, sounding amazed. "I didn't realize you liked older guys."

"I never really thought about it before. I just like who I like. But there's something about him that just got to me. Yeah, he's older, but he also seemed really shy. Almost as if he didn't have much experience. I'm afraid that if things do continue, though, my dad might not be as understanding."

"I don't think you're giving your dad enough credit," Neil said. "Do you really think that he's gonna give you shit for seeing a guy that's a few years older than you?"

"I hope not, but I really don't know for sure. And thirteen years is definitely more than 'a few.' All I know is that I'm not gonna say anything to anyone else just yet—Jon and I agreed to keep in touch, but I have no idea if he really meant it."

Just then, Kyle's phone buzzed. Glancing at the message that popped up on the screen, he turned to Neil and smiled.

"It's him, isn't it?" Neil asked.

"Yeah." Kyle grinned and felt his cheeks redden. "He says, 'Welcome home. Can I call you tonight?'"

"Well, there's your answer. He definitely meant it when he suggested you keep in touch. Tell him yes, lover boy."

Kyle quickly sent off a text. "I told him I was on my way home and that I'd talk to him later."

"Sweet. And really, Kyle, if you're truly serious about this guy, I hope you can make it work."

"Me too, Neil. Me too."

<hr>

AFTER NEIL DROPPED him off at his condo, Kyle unpacked and started a load of laundry. Since he hadn't really slept on the flight home, he set an alarm for five o'clock and quickly fell asleep. When his alarm woke him a few hours later, he felt a bit disoriented, and it took him a moment to remember that he was back home in DC.

Shaking his head at his muddled brain, he moved laundry from the washer to the dryer and started another load. He ambled into the kitchen and noted that the only food he had was in the freezer, so he called and ordered the Buffalo shrimp appetizer and a Signature Burger from Logan Tavern. Then donning his winter coat, he grabbed his phone and keys and walked to the restaurant to get his dinner.

The brisk air felt good, and he quickly got his food and returned home. He reminded himself to stop and get groceries the next day unless he planned to eat out a lot that week.

Kyle was just about to dig into a couple of the shrimp when his phone rang. "Hi, Neil," he said, answering the call.

"Did he call yet?" Neil asked.

"No. I imagine he'll call a bit later. When we parted at the airport, I told him I'd probably crash since I didn't expect to sleep much on the plane."

"Ah, okay. What are you doing?"

"I've got laundry going, and I just got back from picking up a takeout order from Logan Tavern. For some reason, I'm feeling a bit nervous about Jon calling, though," Kyle confessed. "I really don't know why, but I might open some wine to go with my dinner; it might help calm me down a bit."

"As long as you don't overdo it. Remember, tomorrow's a workday. I won't keep you, but call me after your call with Jon. I wanna know how it goes, and I won't last until the morning."

Kyle laughed lightly and said, "I will. Now, let me get back to my dinner, please."

KYLE WAS JUST PUTTING away the leftovers when his phone rang. As he picked up the phone, he saw it was a FaceTime call from Jon. Grabbing his half-full glass of malbec, he walked to the sofa and clicked the Answer button.

"Hi, Jon," he said, getting comfortable. "How are you doing?"

"I'm better now that I'm looking at you," Jon replied. "Is this a good time?"

Kyle smiled broadly and said, "It's perfect actually. I just finished dinner a few minutes ago."

"Oh, good. I wasn't exactly sure what time I should call. Probably should have discussed that earlier."

"Maybe, but it worked out. After I got home, I started some laundry, then crashed for a couple of hours. When I woke up, I realized I didn't have any food in the house, so I got takeout from a place not too far from here." Kyle paused for a moment, collecting his thoughts. "So, that kind of sums up my day; what have you been up to?"

"I managed to sleep on the plane, so I didn't nap when I got home, but like you, I did throw some clothes in the washer. My mom left some chicken enchiladas in my refrigerator with a note welcoming me home and telling me she made me dinner, but she's in her apartment over the garage, so I haven't seen her yet. I know I need to talk to her, but I'm not ready for that today."

"I don't envy you that task," Kyle said. "But you did talk to her and your sister, Bernadette, on Christmas Day, so it's not like you haven't spoken to her since you left Phoenix a couple of weeks ago."

"True, but there's still that crazy elephant in the room— she doesn't like the fact that I'm gay but wants me to meet someone so that I can start a family. I just can't deal with that right now. I think I need to talk to Bernie before I actually confront my mom although I don't imagine us seeing things the same way anytime soon."

"Well, if there's anything I can do to help, please let me know. Even if it's just someone to vent to. I know you're in a difficult position."

"Thanks, Kyle. I appreciate that. I know we haven't known each other for very long, but you're a great guy, and I'm really glad we got to know each other a bit in England."

"I feel the same way, Jon. To be honest, when you said you wanted to keep in touch once we got back home, I wasn't sure if you really meant that, but I'm hoping this call means you really do want to stay connected." Kyle paused, not knowing how much more he should say at that point. *Ah well, in for a penny, in for a pound* ... He barreled on, "You were an unexpected surprise at Christmas, and I really want to get to know you better. I'd like to see where this thing goes … if that's okay with you."

"I'd like that too," Jon agreed. "I wasn't expecting to meet anyone at all, let alone someone like you, but yeah, I'd like to see if we can make this work."

There was a lull in the conversation, and Jon yawned. "Gee, Jon," Kyle said. "It looks like your lack of a nap is catching up to you. You must be beat. Why don't we pick up this conversation in a day or two when we're both more rested? Even though it's still pretty early here, I expect that I'll crash before too long, and I really need to be alert on my first day back to work tomorrow."

"That's a great idea," Jon agreed. "I didn't realize how tired I was, but now that you mention it, I'm probably going to hit the sack as soon as we get off this call."

"Okay then, sleep well, Jon, and I'll talk to you soon." Before he realized what he was doing, Kyle had blown him a kiss.

"You too." Jon smiled and repeated the action. "Good night."

CHAPTER 2

"What the hell am I even doing, trying to get to know Kyle better? I must be crazy," Jon said, shaking his head. "I mean, he can do so much better than me. And let's not even get into the age thing. I'm thirteen years older than him, for fuck's sake."

"Don't even go there, Jon. You're a catch even if you can't see it. And age is just a number, so toss that right outta your head." Teresa stared at him pointedly. "You know I don't like it when you talk shit like that about yourself."

Teresa was another paralegal at the firm where Jon worked, and she'd been his best friend for several years. They'd just finished putting together some files for an upcoming case and had decided to reward themselves with a

15

cup of coffee in the break room. Fortunately, their coworkers were serious about their coffee, so there was always a fresh pot. "I'm sorry, T. I just don't understand what Kyle sees in me. My life is pretty fucked up; why would he want any part of that?"

"Seriously, Jon? You're a handsome guy, and you're fun to be with. And apparently Kyle likes older guys, or he wouldn't have given you the time of day. Why wouldn't he be interested in you?" She paused, looking like a lightbulb had just gone off. "Wait, when I spoke to you yesterday, you said you were going to call him. Did you talk to him?"

"Yeah. I wanted to call him right away but forced myself to wait a bit, figuring that he'd probably crash when he got home. The call was nice, and he says he's interested in seeing where this goes, but I still think that he's gonna smarten up at some point and tell me that it just won't work out between us."

"I call bullshit."

Jon laughed. He loved how Teresa pulled no punches and just told it like it was.

"Furthermore," she continued, "I'd disagree with you about your life being fucked up. Your family, maybe, but not your whole life." She chuckled. "And show me anyone with a family that isn't at least a little crazy. We've all got skeletons in our closets, my friend."

"I guess you're right. With my family, there's no 'maybe' about it. I mean, I love my mom, but she's batshit crazy, T. Plus, I may have let Kyle believe I was a bit more experienced than I really am. And let's not forget that my ex rides the crazy train too. I've got more baggage than most—I'm sure once Kyle realizes how much, he'll dump me in record time. And I can't say I'll blame him."

"I concede that your ex is a total wing nut," Teresa agreed, "but you finally smartened up and dumped him, so at least that craziness is gone from your life."

"I'd like to think so, but you know as well as I do, T, Dylan didn't take it well when I broke up with him. I might be paranoid, but something in the back of my head says that I haven't seen the last of him." Jon sighed.

"I pray that you're wrong about that."

"Me too," Jon agreed. He stood and rinsed his cup at the sink. "Now, let's get back to work. I still have some research to do on the Perkins case."

AT FIVE FORTY-FIVE THAT AFTERNOON, Teresa poked her head into the conference room where Jon sat surrounded by a few file boxes, reading though a thick document. Several folders and a yellow legal pad were in front of him on the mahogany table.

Jon and Teresa shared a small office just down the hall, but there wasn't much space to spread out there, so they often ended up commandeering the conference space to work more comfortably.

"You're not gonna stay here all night, are you?" she asked.

"No." Jon sighed. He took off his reading glasses and looked up at her. "I've had it for today."

"Great. Wanna join me for a drink at Pigtails?" The bar was a short walk from their office and a favorite spot for an after-work drink and sometimes a bite to eat.

Jon glanced at his watch. "Wow, I didn't realize the time.

But in answer to your question, yes. A drink is exactly what I need after spending the afternoon with all this." He gestured to the files and boxes surrounding him. "Let me just pack up some of this, and we can head out."

"Okay, do you need help with anything?" Teresa queried.

"That would be great." Packing the folders into one of the boxes, Jon handed it to her along with the legal pad. "If you can take this into our office and just stick it on my desk, I'll grab these others and stick them in the corner of the office. That way, they're ready for me in the morning."

PIGTAILS WAS TYPICALLY CROWDED at that hour, but a few minutes after they arrived, a couple of spots opened up at the bar, and they settled there. After ordering their drinks, Teresa turned to him. "Okay, so to pick up our conversation where we left off earlier today, you spoke to Kyle last night, and he said he was interested in you. So, what happens now?"

Jon chuckled and shook his head. "Of course, you're not gonna let this go, are you?"

"C'mon, Jon." Teresa grinned. "You know me better than that."

Jon thought back to when they had first met. Teresa had been hired about a year after Jon, and he'd been asked to show her around and explain how things typically worked at the office. They hit it off immediately. He loved her quick wit and how she said what was on her mind. A few months after she was hired, the firm expanded a bit more, and they started sharing an office. He thought they complemented each other well, and over time, T, as he often called her, had become more like a sister to him.

"Yeah, I certainly do know that you wouldn't drop it. Kyle didn't exactly say he was interested in me, just that he wanted to see where this thing might go, and I agreed."

"Well, honey, if he wants to see where this is going, I'd have to say that he's definitely interested in you."

At that point, the bartender brought their drinks over, giving Jon a moment to gather his thoughts.

"Okay, I see your point. But what happens when he realizes that I'm inexperienced and a mess, and he wants nothing more to do with me?" Jon said quietly. "I must admit that I don't really feel worthy of someone like him."

"Now, why do you think that, Jon? I get that Dylan did a number on you and your self-esteem but explain these feelings to me. You admitted that you don't know Kyle all that well, but you've already decided that he's too good for you. Why?"

"He just seems to have it all together. First of all, he's gorgeous. A few inches shorter than me, with dirty-blond hair that has a touch of red in it when the sun hits it just right. And these amazing green eyes." Jon smiled and pulled out his phone, showing T a photo that he'd taken of Kyle at Christmastime. "But it's not just his looks. He comes across as really self-confident, and his dad and uncle are both very successful. His dad's a famous actor, for God's sake—Ben freakin' Rockingham—why would Kyle be interested in someone like me?"

"I don't know, Jon; maybe because you're hot and intelligent and successful and, oh, did I mention hot?" Teresa grinned widely.

Jon's shoulders relaxed a little, and he smiled back. "Okay, I get it. How do you do that?"

"I just keep telling you the truth until it finally sinks into that thick head of yours. Sometimes, it takes longer than others, but I don't give up. And you shouldn't either, Jon. It sounds like Kyle might be just what you need. Instead of fighting it and dooming the whole thing from the start, why don't you figure out how you can gently discuss those things that scare you: your crazy-ass mama, your super-crazy ex, and your supposed lack of experience? You might find that if there's really something between the two of you, those things won't seem so bad, and Kyle might even be able to help you deal with some of the shit going on in your life."

"I don't know what I did to deserve you in my life, T, but I'm thankful every day for you. Drinks are on me today," Jon replied.

"Works for me." Teresa caught the bartender's eye and said, "Another round, please."

CHAPTER 3

Thursday, December 31 – New Year's Eve

K yle didn't have any plans for New Year's Eve—sure, there were places he could go and celebrate with anonymous people, but he wasn't really in the mood to party. The office was closing at three, so he talked about it with Neil at lunchtime. Since neither of them had plans, Kyle had invited Neil over for a late dinner. They'd open a bottle of Champagne and watch the ball drop and call it a night. And if they ended up having a bit too much to drink, Neil could stay in the guest room.

Since returning home, Kyle and Jon had chatted every day. Things still seemed tense between Jon and his mom, but Jon didn't say too much about it, and Kyle didn't want to pry. Kyle wanted to give Jon space and figured that he'd say more when he was ready. They mostly talked about work and slowly began to share more things about themselves. Kyle acknowledged that while he had a few friends in DC, Neil was his closest, and he looked forward to Jon meeting him at some point. Jon confessed that he didn't have a lot of friends but spent most of his time with either T or his sister, Bernadette, whom he'd called Bernie since they were kids.

At just past seven thirty, Kyle was in the kitchen putting the final touches on a green salad when his doorbell rang. Neil held not one but two bottles of prosecco, which they both preferred over Champagne. "Looks like it's gonna be a happy New Year for sure," Kyle said, eyeing the bottles. "I have two bottles in the fridge as well."

"We don't have to drink all of them, but I figured it's best to be prepared," Neil retorted. His two bottles joined those in the fridge. "Ooh, is that lasagna?" Neil asked, spotting the casserole on the shelf next to the wine.

"Yeah, I found some sauce in the freezer, so I made my dad's recipe. I know it's a lot of carbs, but we deserve it. Can you stick the salad in there too, please?"

"What time are we gonna eat?" Neil asked.

"I'll put the lasagna in the oven in about a half hour, so we'll eat around nine. If you're feeling hungry, we can have some cheese and crackers to tide us over. And if you want to start in on the prosecco, take a bottle out now."

Kyle prepped some snacks while Neil poured each of them a flute of the sparkling wine, and they got comfortable in the living room. "Did Jon call you yet?"

"No, we texted earlier, and he said he'd call tonight, but we didn't actually set a time. Would you like to meet him? I mean, the two of you will eventually meet in person at some point, but I thought I could introduce you over FaceTime tonight."

"That would be nice," Neil agreed. "But don't worry, I'll make myself scarce after the introductions so you two can play virtual kissy face or whatever it is that you do." Neil winked.

"Okay, we might throw each other a kiss, especially since it's New Year's Eve, but we don't do anything else when we chat." Kyle hesitated, then looked shyly at Neil. "At least not yet."

"Ha, but you're hoping that happens at some point, you devil!" Neil laughed.

"I already told you that we did some things Christmas night. I certainly wouldn't say no to doing a few things remotely," Kyle admitted. "But despite our antics in England, Jon seems rather shy at times, so I'm not going to push him to do anything. I want him to feel comfortable, so I'm playing it by ear."

"Fair enough. I'm not judging, you know. If anything, I'm just a bit jealous."

"Speaking of ... whatever happened to that guy you saw a few times before the holidays; Tristan, was it?"

"Oh my God, I forgot to tell you. You left for England, and we only just texted a few times, so I never got to tell you what happened with that bastard," Neil replied.

"Oh no!" Kyle exclaimed. "Do tell."

"As you know, I had taken a few extra days off before the holiday so I could finish my shopping, and I planned to leave Wednesday morning to drive to my mom's house. I had agreed to meet Tristan for brunch on Tuesday at Ted's Bulletin since we wouldn't see each other for Christmas." Neil shook his head. "I still can't believe this happened. We were having mimosas, and I was telling him about what Christmas with the Watkins clan is like, when this striking blonde woman walked up to our table and said, 'Is this why you couldn't stay last night, Tris? Didn't want to be late for brunch with him?'"

"Fuck," Kyle uttered. "It gets worse, doesn't it?"

Neil nodded, sadness clear in his eyes. "Tristan started to say, 'But baby, I can explain …' But she cut him off, slapped him across the face, threw what was left of his mimosa at him, and practically shrieked, 'The engagement is off!' as she stormed out of the restaurant."

"Oh. My. God. Neil, I'm so sorry."

"Needless to say, I got up as calmly as I could and walked out. Sure, we'd only gone out a few times and weren't exclusive or anything, but a fiancée? Seriously? I didn't care that he was bi, but an engagement usually means you're not seeing anyone else. Why do these things happen to me?"

"Shit, Neil, I didn't mean to bring up bad memories," Kyle said sympathetically.

"It's fine, really. I went home, cried for about twenty minutes, then concluded that it was for the best and moved on. Frankly, I'm glad that it happened that early in our relationship. It's not like I thought he was 'the one' or anything, and I hadn't fallen for him. It was crappy that it was just before Christmas, but thankfully, I got to spend time with my family, and that helped me put Tristan out of my mind."

"I'm sorry I wasn't around for you, but as you said, you had your family, and I know they're a good distraction." Kyle knew that Neil's sister's three kids loved their uncle, and Christmas was surely a fun time for all.

"Enough talking about my dismal love life. Pour me some more prosecco and stick that lasagna in the oven already."

———

THE LASAGNA HAD ABOUT fifteen more minutes in the oven, and the first bottle of prosecco was empty when Kyle's phone rang. He glanced at the screen and saw that it was Jon, so he picked up his iPad to answer the FaceTime call.

"Hey, Jon."

"Hi, Kyle. How are you doing? Getting ready to go out and celebrate?"

"No, I wasn't in a party mood, so I invited Neil to come over for dinner. We've already managed to polish off one bottle of prosecco." He lifted his glass, toasted Jon, then took a sip.

"Well, cheers to you both," Jon replied. "I wish I was there celebrating with you."

"How about you? Are you going out to celebrate tonight?" Kyle asked.

"No, Mom was in a mood, so I offered to babysit for Bernie so she and her husband could go out. The kids are in bed, so it's just me and some beer as I watch all the lunatics in Times Square on TV."

"I wish you were here too, Jon. But you're a good uncle, and I'm sure Bernie appreciates that." Kyle paused and gestured to Neil to come closer. "Jon Rivera, I want you to meet Neil Watkins, my best friend and partner in crime at work. Neil, this is Jon."

"Pleased to meet you, Jon," Neil said.

"Likewise, Neil," replied Jon. "Kyle's told me a lot about you. Hope we can meet in person someday."

"Definitely, Jon. You'll have to come to DC for a visit."

"I'd like that," Jon agreed.

"Okay, I'm gonna go into Kyle's spare room and call my family in Virginia to wish them a happy New Year—and give you some private time. It was great meeting you, Jon."

"Same, Neil. Happy New Year."

Neil left, and Kyle said, "So, how was your day? I'm surprised you're not with T tonight."

"Work was okay, and T made plans with a couple of girlfriends to have a New Year's slumber party. I'm really happy to be able to watch Bernie's kids for her, though. And T's coming over to my place tomorrow afternoon. We'll drink beer and watch football together."

"Sounds nice. I do really wish you were here, though. I know we saw each other less than a week ago, but it would be nice to spend more time together," Kyle affirmed, surprising himself. He usually wasn't that open about his feelings, especially so soon into a relationship. He figured it must be the wine.

"Speaking of spending more time together," Jon started, "it looks like I'm gonna be going to a conference in Albuquerque in February. I don't have all the specifics yet, but it ends on the Friday before Presidents' Day. Would you consider flying out on that Friday and spending the long weekend with me?"

"Really? Albuquerque, huh? Yeah, I'd like that," Kyle said with a smile.

"Cool. I'll admit I was a bit afraid to ask, but I really do want to see you again, and this seemed like the perfect opportunity."

"It is. Text me whatever details you have, and I'll see about taking that Friday off."

"I will. Okay, I'll let you get back to dinner with Neil. Happy New Year, Kyle." Jon blew him a kiss, dipping his head shyly.

"Happy New Year to you, Jon," Kyle replied and blew back his own kiss.

CHAPTER 4

Friday, January 1 – New Year's Day, Jon's house

Jon was taking the pigs in a blanket out of the oven when he heard the side door open. Teresa walked in with a large carryout bag.

"I come bearing wings," she announced as she walked into the kitchen. "Oh, and Happy New Year."

"Happy New Year to you too, T," Jon replied.

For the past couple of years, Jon and Teresa had gotten together on New Year's Day to eat wings and drink beer and talk. They might say they were going to watch football, but while some game invariably was playing on the large flat-screen TV in Jon's living room, they never really saw much of the action, preferring to spend their time chatting about a variety of subjects.

"So how was babysitting duty last night?" Teresa asked.

"Fine. I got there in time for dinner with the kids, and we watched a little TV once Bernie and Jeff left for their evening out. The kids went to bed without too much trouble, then I read for a while, drank some beer, and managed to stay awake to watch the downtown Phoenix midnight festivities on television. I crashed about fifteen minutes later."

"Oh, I didn't realize you were planning to stay over," T said.

"Yeah, it was just easier. And even though it's a short drive home, I don't really like being out on the road—too many crazies out there. I had breakfast with everyone this morning and got home about an hour ago. Did you have fun at your slumber party?"

Jon opened the bag that Teresa had brought and found two containers of chicken wings—Honey BBQ and Buffalo—complete with a container of blue cheese dressing and some celery sticks. He piled them up on two plates and added them to the pigs in a blanket and chips and salsa that were on the kitchen island.

"Oh my God, we had so much fun!" Teresa exclaimed. "I don't get to hang out with those girls often enough, so it's always a gab fest when we get together. We ate way too much, but surprisingly, I didn't drink all that much. Oh well, I'll probably make up for that today."

"Yeah, you say that, but you'll have a couple of beers and then switch to water or club soda or something. And speaking of beer ... here." Jon took two beers out of the fridge and handed one to her.

"I may surprise you today. Since we don't have to work tomorrow, I might just let loose."

"You know you can always stay over if you don't want to drive home," Jon told her.

"Yeah, and I appreciate that," Teresa replied. "By the way, did you talk to Kyle last night?"

"Yeah. I called him right after I got the kids settled. He invited his friend Neil over for dinner, so I got to meet him last night. He seems like a great guy."

"Ah, so no video sexy times with your guy, huh?" Teresa teased.

"Hmmm, not that we do those things, but no. But I did do something a little out of character for me," Jon admitted.

"Oh, really? What did you do?" T teased. "C'mon, Jon, spill."

"You know that conference I'm going to in Albuquerque next month? It ends on the Friday before the long weekend, so I worked up the courage and asked Kyle if he'd be interested in coming in on that Friday so we can spend the weekend together." Jon smiled, feeling pleased with himself.

"Good for you, Jon," Teresa said. "I know that wasn't easy for you. So, what did he say?"

"He said yes!" Jon blew out a large breath. "I was kinda scared to ask him, and part of me was expecting him to say no, but I'm glad I went with my gut this time."

"Yay! That's excellent, Jon."

"I know that there are still a lot of things that Kyle and I need to talk about, and I don't want to get my hopes up, but it feels right, so I'm gonna try and not overthink things."

LATER THAT EVENING

. . .

Jon had called it; T had switched to club soda after about two and a half beers. She'd left about twenty minutes earlier, and Jon was wiping down the kitchen counter after loading up the dishwasher. His phone rang, and glancing at the screen, he saw his sister's photo.

"Hey, Bernie, what's up?"

"Have you talked to Mama today?" she asked.

"No," Jon admitted. "I've kind of been avoiding her. I'm still really upset at the things she said to me before Christmas."

"Oh, you mean when you just ran off to Sam and then to England, letting me deal with her crap?" Bernie replied, the anger clear in her voice.

"I'm sorry, sis, I thought we talked about this, and you understood what I was feeling," Jon said, a bit confused.

"You're right, and I'm sorry." Bernie sighed. "Mama just called me and started spewing the same shit all over again, and it just kind of got to me. She said that she doesn't understand why you like men, but if that's how you're gonna be, the least you could do is find someone to start a family with, and I quote, 'before it's too late.'"

"Before what's too late?" Jon sputtered. "What if I don't want to start a family?"

"Not only that, but what about my freakin' family? I mean, doesn't that count for something?" Bernie said, clearly exasperated. "I know she loves the kids, but I always get the feeling that they're somehow not enough."

"I've been thinking about it, and as crazy as it sounds, I think it may have something to do with the fact that your kids have Jeff's name, and she expects me to have kids in order to continue the Rivera name," Jon replied.

"Seriously? Do you think that's it?" Bernie asked. "That's really fucked up, you know."

"You're right, it is fucked up, but that's all I've been able to come up with," Jon confirmed. "Mom's always been pretty traditional, but it seemed to get worse after Papa died. And the older she gets, the worse it gets."

"You're right, it is worse than it used to be. Do you think you might be able to talk to her and explain it in a way that she'll understand?" Bernie asked. "I've tried more than once, but I can't seem to get anywhere with her. I don't know what else to do."

"Okay, I'll see if I can figure something out. I know I can't keep avoiding her; that's just the cowardly thing to do, and it doesn't solve anything." Jon paused for a moment. He had wanted to tell Bernie about Kyle but hadn't really found a good time since he'd returned home. Maybe this was it.

"So, Bernie ..." he began, "there's something I've been wanting to tell you."

"Oh my God, you've met someone, haven't you?" she said excitedly.

"How the fuck do you do that?" Jon replied, flabbergasted.

"I'm your sister, silly," she said jokingly. "But seriously, there was something different about you when you got back from visiting Samantha. Is it somebody in Massachusetts? A friend of hers? Oh, wait, did you meet someone in England? I want to know everything."

"Okay, but are you sure you have time?" Jon joked, knowing there was no way she'd end the call without knowing all the details. "Don't you have to get the kids ready for bed or something?" he added innocently.

"Nice try, Jon," Bernie said. "Just get on with it."

He chuckled. "Remember Sam's friend Rob?"

"Yeah, he's the one who went on that cruise about a year ago and met Ben Rockingham, and they fell in love. You said that the house in England where you stayed belongs to Ben's family, right?"

"Exactly. It seems that this was a family Christmas with Ben's brother and sister-in-law, his son, and Ben's assistant. Remember, Sam brought me along when I showed up unexpectedly on her doorstep after I had that blowout with Mom," Jon explained. "Anyway, Ben's son, Kyle, and I kind of hit it off while we were there."

"That's great, Jon!" Bernie exclaimed. "They're Sam's friends, so they've got to be good people. What's he like? When can I meet him?"

"Slow down, sis." Jon laughed. "We just met over Christmas, and he lives in DC ..." Jon hesitated.

"Okay, but I sense that there's something you're not telling me," Bernie said.

"Um, yeah, about that, well, he's, um ..." Jon paused, hoping that Bernie wouldn't freak out. "He's younger than me."

"So that shouldn't be ... wait a minute. How much younger?"

"Thirteen years, sis. This is crazy, right?"

"Hey, Jeff is almost nine years older than me, so I don't think it's as bad as you're making it seem. And it's not like he's eighteen or anything. But I can tell this is freaking you out, right?"

"A little," Jon acknowledged. "Kyle doesn't seem to mind, but he's afraid his dad will have a major problem with it."

"I can understand that," said Bernie. "But surely Sam could help since she knows Ben a bit better than you."

"Well, see, Sam doesn't actually know about Kyle and me. We spent some time together in England, mostly with other people around. But we did go off for a walk together, and, um, we kinda hooked up on Christmas night."

"Aha! I knew there was something different about you. You got some on your little trip." There was clearly a smile in Bernie's voice when she spoke. "I'm happy for you, brother."

"Um, thanks? This conversation has gotten weird. I'm really not used to talking to you about my sex life. Anyway, we talked about it and decided not to say anything until we see if this is going to go anywhere. Once we're sure about that, Kyle will figure out how to tell his dad about us. But until then, you can't say anything to anyone, including Mom and Sam. Okay?"

"My lips are sealed, Jon," Bernie promised. "But I'm thinking that you're already all in on this thing with Kyle, right?"

"Ahem," Jon started, "yes and no. I mean, I really do like him. He's smart and handsome and can be quite serious although he's also a lot of fun. Part of me is already falling for him, but I'm also afraid, sis."

"Oh, Jon, sweetie, what are you afraid of?" Bernie asked quietly.

"That eventually, Kyle is gonna realize that I'm a fucking mess and will drop me so damn fast. I'm not sure my heart can take it. As much as I want him, it might just be easier if I walk away first. That way it won't hurt so much."

"If I ever see that fucking Dylan again, I'll rip his balls off!" Bernie exclaimed, venom dripping from her words. "He did a number on you for sure. You're not a mess, Jon. That asshole tried to convince you of that, but it's because he's so insecure."

"Part of me knows that, Bern, but part of me still isn't convinced," Jon confessed. "I've actually been thinking about calling that therapist I saw a few years ago. I think maybe talking with someone about the crap that Dylan put me through and the fact that I'm now seeing Kyle may help me put it all into perspective."

"That's a really good idea, Jon. You need someone who can be objective about everything, and they helped you before, right?" Bernie asked.

"They did," Jon agreed. "I'll call and see if I can get an appointment. It would also be nice to have someone to talk to about Mom. She's been acting so crazy lately. Kyle at least knows part of that story since we talked a little bit about it in England. What must he think about all the craziness in my life?"

"If he knows even part of Mom's story and he's still interested in talking to you and, well, um, doing other things with you ..." Jon blushed at her words and was glad it wasn't a video call. "Then I think you already have your answer about that," Bernie continued. "He's definitely interested, and whatever Mom is dealing with doesn't matter to him."

"Thanks, sis. I love you. Thanks for your support; you don't know how much that means to me."

"I love you too, baby brother." Jon grinned. She was only a year older than him, but she always had his back. "Okay. I'll let you go now; gotta see how Jeff's making out with getting the kids in bed. I'll talk to you tomorrow."

Jon sighed as he hung up the phone. Bernie was right; it wasn't as bad as he was making it out to be. But that wasn't always easy for him to believe. He'd just have to try harder.

***

THE FOLLOWING *week*

JON KNOCKED on the door to his mom's in-law apartment, located above the garage. He'd installed an elevator for her a couple of years before, but out of habit, he always used the stairs to reach her door.

"*Hola, hijo,*" Louisa said when she opened the door. "Come in."

As Jon walked in, he leaned down and gave her a hug. "I'm sorry, Mama. I've been avoiding you, and that was wrong." Louisa Rivera was a tiny woman with short, salt-and-pepper hair and dark-brown eyes. She hugged him back tightly.

"It's okay, Jon," she replied. "I know I said things that upset you, and I'm sorry too. I know we don't see eye to eye about a lot of things, and I may have a bit of a temper."

Jon laughed. "A bit of a temper, Mama? You're fierce!"

That brought a smile to her face. "Your papa always said that to me."

"I remember that," Jon agreed. "That's kind of why I said it. So, Mama, there's something I want to talk to you about."

"Okay, *hijo*, do you want some coffee? I just made a pot."

"Sure, that would be nice." Louisa prepared two cups, and they sat in her cozy living room.

"What do you want to talk about, son?"

"Well, Ma, it's like this," Jon began. "I know that you don't like the fact that I'm gay, but it's not gonna change. This is who I am. But then you got upset that Dylan and I broke up; that didn't make sense to me. No one in the family seemed to like him, and frankly, the more I got to know him, the more I found out he was a real jerk. When I finally realized how bad he was, I ended it. He wasn't good for me."

"You're right, Jon. I don't really understand why you are the way you are, and yes, it bothers me. I wish your father was still here to help me with this. Did we do something wrong when you were growing up? Is this our fault?" Louisa's voice trembled a bit, and Jon thought she might start to cry.

"No, Mama!" he cried. "You and Papa didn't do anything wrong. It's not your fault because there's nothing wrong with me. I know it's not easy for you, Ma, and I will do what I can to help you understand, but it's okay. I'm happy with who I am."

"Okay, *hijo*," Louisa said. "While you were gone, I thought a lot about what I said, and I guess I need to think more about this, but I'll leave it for now. And if that Dylan wasn't good for you, then good riddance. My son deserves better. Now look, Jon," she added sternly, "you're not getting any younger and neither am I. When are you gonna find someone that you can settle down with so I can have some more *nietos*?"

Jon smiled. It seemed his mom had a one-track mind. "Mama, is this about carrying on the Rivera name?" he asked gently. "Because even if I do meet someone, and, as you put it, 'settle down,' that doesn't mean I'll start a family."

"But *hijo*, families are always better with lots of *niños*," Louisa replied.

"Mama, we'll just have to agree to disagree for now. If it happens, fine, but I can't promise that I'll find someone and settle down and have lots of *niños* just so that you're happy. Understand?" He thought about saying something about Kyle to his mom but realized it was still a bit too early. Maybe in a few months if things were still going well between him and Kyle.

"Okay, Jon," she agreed, smiling slyly. "But we'll talk about this again."

CHAPTER 5

Wednesday, January 13 – Kyle's office

K yle was in his office, finishing up some notes on a client's portfolio. It was almost lunchtime, and he was looking forward to finally hanging out with Neil. Work had been hectic lately, and they hadn't spent much time together since New Year's Eve.

Kyle reflected on how far he and Neil had come with the company. They'd moved up the ranks in the firm together and were both now senior financial analysts. They worked for different account managers but had offices right next to each other and were at a point in their careers where they were handling portfolios for a few clients. Kyle enjoyed the work, understood the markets, and was a whiz with numbers. Both his clients and his manager seemed to think he was doing a good job, and that make Kyle happy.

At one o'clock, Kyle got up and left his office. Neil's door was open, so Kyle stuck his head in and said, "Are you ready to grab lunch?"

"Yeah, let me just finish this email. It'll only take a minute," Neil replied. As Neil typed, Kyle studied him. He was classically handsome, with dark-brown hair and striking blue eyes. He worked out, and it showed: with wide shoulders and a trim waist, he stood several inches taller than Kyle's five foot seven. Some days, Kyle wished they had clicked as more than friends, but he then quickly realized he treasured Neil's friendship far more than the idea of sex. Hopefully, this thing with Jon would turn into something.

"Okay, I'm ready," Neil said as he shrugged into his topcoat.

"Where do you want to go?"

"How about Teaism? I can eat a bit healthier there, and after everything I consumed over the holidays, I need that for a change."

BY THE TIME they got there, the restaurant wasn't overly crowded, and they only had to wait a couple of minutes for a table.

Once they'd ordered, Kyle said, "So, how are things? Even though we commute to and from work together, it feels like we haven't actually talked for ages."

"I know, right? Neither one of us has been in a very chatty mood on the Metro lately," Neil agreed. "I'm doing okay. Needless to say, I haven't met anyone new since I have no life at the moment. Frankly, I'm tired of getting in early and working until almost eight o'clock each night. I thought we paid our dues when we first started, and things were supposed to get better."

Kyle laughed in agreement. "It's gonna be okay. The company had a bit of a growth spurt, and we're all dealing with it. But I heard Mr. Jameson say that they were working on hiring some new folks and taking over more office space on the eleventh floor. It should start easing up in the next couple of weeks."

"I hope you're right." Changing the subject, Neil asked, "So, how are things going with Jon?"

"Really, really good," Kyle answered, his smile wide. "We text every day and video chat regularly. He really is a great guy although he is a bit insecure."

"He's insecure? I'd think an older guy would have his shit together."

"Me too. But apparently, he hasn't really dated all that much, and his ex sounds like a real dick. From the little that Jon has said, this Dylan guy did a number on him. But he started seeing his old therapist again, and he said that's helping."

"Good. No one's perfect, and if he's doing something about it, that says something about him and the fact that he wants to move forward."

"Exactly what I told him. Hey, did I tell you that I'm going to see him in about a month?"

"Um, I vaguely remember something about that, but I can't recall the details. You're going to Phoenix?"

"No, Jon is going to a conference on family law in Albuquerque and asked me to meet him for the weekend. His conference ends on Friday of the long weekend, so I'll fly out Friday afternoon and come home on Monday."

"That's great, Kyle. It sounds like things are working out well for the two of you."

"It feels right," Kyle agreed. "But that also means that I'll need to talk to my dad and Rob about him. But I'll probably wait until after the weekend in New Mexico just be sure that Jon and I are on the same page about this relationship. I know I'm not seeing anyone else at this point, and Jon isn't either. We just kind of became a couple although we haven't used words like 'boyfriend' yet." Kyle smiled wistfully. "But that's how I think of him, ya know?"

"Oh yeah, I can see it on your face when you talk about him," Neil agreed. "Perhaps that's something the two of you should talk about, huh?"

"You're right. That's definitely something we need to discuss."

Jon was reading a new book on his Kindle when his phone rang. He picked it up from the end table and saw Kyle's photo on the screen. He grabbed his iPad instead and opened the FaceTime app.

"Hey, handsome," he said once he saw Kyle's smiling face on the screen. "What's going on?"

"Hi, Jon. I just finished cleaning up after dinner and decided that I wanted to talk to you. How was your day?"

"Good. Work was work, but I was busy, so it flew by. How are things with you?"

"Okay. I had lunch with Neil today, and we started talking about you and me," Kyle replied.

"Hmm, okay. Should I be worried?" Jon asked, feeling a bit uneasy.

"Not at all, it's just that while Neil and I were chatting, I realized that we've never really said what we are. We got to know each other a bit at Christmastime, and we did, um, other things too." Kyle's blush was visible on the screen. "And we've kept on seeing each other long-distance."

"Okay," Jon said, wondering where this might be going. "Are you asking to be my boyfriend, Kyle?" He grinned.

"Maybe," Kyle admitted. "I guess, yeah. Um, I mean, we are boyfriends at this point, right?"

Jon's eyes twinkled, and he chuckled. "Yeah, I guess we are. That's okay, right?"

"More than okay," said Kyle. "As Neil and I talked, I realized that I thought of you as my boyfriend, but you and I really haven't talked about it, and I felt like we needed to. Thank you."

"Of course, sweetie. Is it okay if I call you sweetie?" Jon asked.

"Yes. Absolutely, pookie. No, scratch that. Not pookie." Kyle laughed.

"Whew, good. Not a fan of pookie. So, boyfriend, what happens next?" Jon asked. His smile was wide, and he had a twinkle in his eyes.

"Well, to celebrate making it official, would you be interested in some sexy times?" Kyle asked mischievously.

"Um, you mean ..." Jon was suddenly tongue-tied. "I haven't done anything like that before, but yeah, I'd like that a lot."

"Yes," Kyle cooed. "Maybe we should relocate to our respective bedrooms?"

When Jon got to his room, he saw that Kyle had propped up his iPad so that Jon could see him standing next to his king-size bed. He watched as Kyle unbuttoned his shirt and slowly peeled it off, obviously giving Jon a show. Staring straight into the camera, he popped the button on his jeans and lowered the zipper, revealing black underwear. While Jon favored boxer briefs, Kyle was wearing trunks, and Jon got an eyeful of those tight shorts as Kyle lowered the jeans and stepped out of them. Kyle turned slightly, and his arousal was clear by the bulge in the front of the trunks.

"Are you gonna join me?" Kyle asked seductively.

"Oh, um, yeah," Jon stuttered, leaning his iPad against the bed pillows and pulling his T-shirt over his head.

Kyle's expression revealed that he had noticed that bit of hesitancy on Jon's part. "Hey, we don't have to do this if you're uncomfortable, babe."

Jon smiled shyly and said, "Oh, I want to do this, but it's new to me, so I don't really know what I'm doing." As he spoke, he undid his pants and took them off, leaving him in just a pair of lime-green boxer briefs.

"Wow," Kyle said, smiling at Jon's package, encased in the bright boxers. "Nice underwear, Jon."

"Um, thanks," Jon said, blushing. "They're kinda bright, so I don't wear them very often, but I haven't done laundry yet this week, so I didn't have a lot of options this morning."

"Oh, you definitely need to wear those more often. They look amazing on you," Kyle replied, his voice low and sexy. "But now, I think they'd look better off."

They both removed their underwear and climbed onto their beds.

Holding his iPad in one hand, Kyle moved his free hand down his chest and grabbed his hard cock.

"I wish you were here to do this for me," he said huskily. "I want to feel your hands caress me and your hot mouth on my dick."

Jon groaned. He tried to mimic the position of his iPad to match Kyle's so they both had a close-up view of each other's rigid cocks. He slowly stroked his straining member. "I wish we were together too. I remember how good you felt in my arms on Christmas night."

"Oh yeah," Kyle panted, bending his knees and spreading his legs as he jerked himself more quickly.

Jon matched Kyle stroke for stroke and moaned, "Oh God, I'm close, Kyle."

"That's it. Come for me, babe," Kyle said, his voice almost a whisper. Jon jerked himself faster and faster.

Jon moaned, and he felt his balls tighten. "Oh," he cried, and hot cum hit his chest over and over again.

Kyle grunted and reached his own orgasm. Cum spattered his belly and ran over his hand as he slowed his movements.

"Wow," uttered Jon, "that was intense." He smiled at Kyle as he ran his fingers through the cooling spunk on his chest.

"Yeah, it was," Kyle agreed, grinning back at him. "I almost blacked out for a second."

"We definitely need to do that again sometime," added Jon.

"Definitely," Kyle agreed, "but now we should probably clean up. I don't want to fall asleep like this."

"Yeah, pretty sure I'm going to drop off any minute," Jon said. "I'll talk to you tomorrow, sweetie."

"Sweet dreams, babe."

CHAPTER 6

Friday, February 12 – Albuquerque, New Mexico

Kyle's flight landed on time at Albuquerque International Sunport, and he quickly made his way out of the building. Since he was just there for the weekend, he only had a small rolling carry-on and his backpack to deal with. Once outside, he used an app on his phone to arrange for a rideshare to the hotel and was surprised to see that the vehicle would be there in just a few minutes. They were never that quick in DC.

Kyle's mind wandered on the drive. Was he doing the right thing, meeting Jon for the weekend? Yeah, he definitely felt something for Jon, and they'd agreed that they were boyfriends, but he kept on getting weird vibes from him. Jon would say things in passing, indicating that he wasn't good enough for Kyle, and sometimes it seemed like he was doing everything he could to try and talk Kyle out of getting involved with him. What was up with that? He was determined to try and talk to Jon about it over the weekend.

After an uneventful ride from the airport, the car pulled up to the entrance of the hotel where Jon was staying, and he got out, bags in hand. As he walked into the lobby, he was surprised to see Jon seated near the front door, obviously keeping an eye out for him.

As soon as Jon spotted Kyle, he got up and hurried toward him. "It's so good to see you," Jon said, hugging him and giving him a peck on the cheek. "How was your flight?"

"It's good to see you too," Kyle replied, returning the kiss. "The flight was fine."

Jon handed him a keycard. "I've got to get to my last seminar of the conference. We're in room 1053. Make yourself at home, and I'll see you in a couple of hours, okay?"

"Sure. I'll drop off my stuff, and then I'll grab a bite to eat. I'll see you soon." They hugged one more time, then Jon headed off to where Kyle assumed the conference facilities were. After dropping his bags in their room, he grabbed his Kindle and went in search of the restaurant.

KYLE HEARD the click of the lock, and he opened his eyes as the door opened, and Jon walked in.

"Hey. Did I wake you?" Jon asked.

"No," Kyle answered. "I was just relaxing but hadn't fallen asleep. Yet." He grinned. "But I might have if you hadn't come in just now."

"Well, it's still early. We have time for a nap if you're tired, and I know I could use one. That last seminar was extremely boring."

Jon loosened his tie as he walked toward the closet. Taking off his suit coat and pants, he hung them in the closet along with his tie. Pulling off his shirt, he tossed it on the floor of the closet and turned to face Kyle, now clad only in navy-blue boxer briefs and socks.

"Now I feel overdressed," Kyle said, lying on the bed in his jeans and gray Henley.

"Well, you could get more comfortable, and we could cuddle under the covers," Jon suggested, a twinkle in his eye.

Kyle grinned and stood up, pulling the Henley over his head, revealing the dark blond smattering of hair on his chest, leading down to his navel and further south. He shucked his jeans and walked toward Jon wearing only forest-green trunks.

They hugged and kissed deeply. "I've missed you," Kyle said. "Now let's get under the covers and start cuddling."

"What a good idea." Jon chuckled. "But let me set an alarm on my phone. We've got a reservation at eight o'clock. There's a tapas restaurant nearby that I thought you might like."

The alarm set, they crawled beneath the covers and hugged once more. One kiss turned into more, and soon their hard lengths were pressed against each other as they moved together, trying to increase the friction. Jon slipped his hand into Kyle's shorts and grasped his hard cock, rubbing his thumb over Kyle's slit.

Kyle moaned into Jon's mouth, sucking on his tongue. His hands dipped into the back of Jon's boxers, and he grabbed Jon's ass cheeks, pulling them apart, then slipping his finger into the crease, searching for Jon's hole. He circled Jon's pucker as Jon pulled Kyle's shorts down, tucking them below his balls as he began to stroke Kyle's throbbing dick more quickly.

"I'm not gonna last if you keep that up." Kyle panted.

"Well, then, let's take care of you … then we can nap." Jon ducked under the covers and swallowed Kyle to the root. Kyle gasped, running his hands through Jon's thick black hair. "Oh God," he gasped.

Quickly throwing off the covers, he spun around and jerked Jon's briefs down, circling the head of Jon's cock with his tongue. He slipped his tongue under Jon's foreskin and ran it along the head of Jon's dick.

As they continued to suck each other's hard cocks, Kyle once again probed Jon's ass in search of his furry hole. Finding his prize, he briefly pulled off Jon's prick so that he could coat his finger with saliva. Taking Jon's dick once again, he teased Jon's hole, then slowly breached him. Jon moaned around Kyle's cock.

Jon's balls tightened up, and Kyle knew he was close. Redoubling his efforts, he felt Jon pull off his dick and breathlessly say, "Gonna come."

Kyle's mouth filled with Jon's orgasm, and he swallowed greedily as he felt his own climax rising to the surface. Letting Jon's cock slip from his lips, he cried, "Coming!" as he spilled into Jon's waiting mouth.

After they'd sucked and licked each other clean, Kyle moved back around and kissed Jon soundly, tasting himself on Jon's tongue. "That was fantastic."

"It was," Jon agreed.

Kyle turned around, becoming the little spoon, and Jon

wrapped his arms around Kyle's chest. As they drifted off to sleep, Kyle couldn't remember the last time he had felt so contented.

———

MÁS TAPAS Y Vino was only a few blocks from their hotel, so they decided to walk. It was a bit chilly, but the fresh air felt good and helped revive them after their nap.

Once seated, they ordered some wine and perused the menu.

"I came here the other night with a few folks from the conference, and the food was amazing. I'm glad I got to come back here with you," Jon said, smiling at Kyle.

"Me too. This all looks fantastic. Anything in particular you recommend?" Kyle asked.

"The *patatas bravas* were really good," Jon said, pointing to it on the menu. "Oh, and the garlic shrimp with chorizo. And you gotta try the honey bacon-wrapped dates."

"Okay, yes to all of those, and I want to try the *empanadas de pollo* too," Kyle agreed. "Let's order those and then see if we need anything else."

"Sounds good."

"I'm really glad you invited me to spend the weekend with you," Kyle said while they waited for their food to arrive. "I've never been to Albuquerque before, and it's been too long since we've been together in person."

"It has," Jon agreed. "I want you to come to Phoenix some-time too, but I know you haven't talked to your dad and Rob yet, and I don't want anything getting back to Sam and messing that up for you."

"I appreciate that, Jon," Kyle replied quietly. "I know I need to talk to both of them, but I guess I've been a bit cowardly about it. I *will* figure out what to say in the next few weeks, and then I'll tell them. Frankly, it's not something I really want to do on the phone or over FaceTime. I'll have to see if I can take a quick trip to see them. It's a short flight from DC, so maybe I can fly up Friday night and then head back home on Sunday."

"Sounds like a plan to me, sweetheart. I don't mean to pressure you at all, but I do think that it will all be so much easier once it's out in the open," Jon said. "I know I felt better after I finally talked to my mom about the tension between us."

"You're absolutely right, Jon."

Just then, their server arrived with some of their food, and they dug in.

CHAPTER 7

Saturday, February 13 – Albuquerque, New Mexico

J on turned over and slowly opened his eyes, quickly shutting them again due to the small gap in the drapes that allowed a blinding swath of sunlight to cut across the bed. He rolled back over toward Kyle and smiled, remembering their time together the night before. It felt good to be with him. Maybe he should stop worrying and just enjoy what was happening. Kyle wasn't at all like Dylan; Kyle was kind and sweet, and he accepted Jon for who he was. Dylan had always made Jon feel like he wasn't good enough.

Jon's bladder reminded him that there was a reason he had woken up, so he carefully rose from the bed, trying hard not to wake Kyle. Walking into the bathroom, he thought about what they could do that day. He'd glanced at the alarm clock on the nightstand and knew it was still rather early, so he thought he'd see if he could go back to sleep for a bit longer. After peeing, he washed his hands and headed back toward the bed.

Kyle's eyes slowly opened. "Hey, babe," he said. "Why are you up already?"

"Nature called," Jon replied, smiling.

"Ah, yeah. I know that feeling. My turn." Kyle got up and padded to the bathroom. He didn't close the door, and Jon could hear him relieving himself.

"Any plans for today?" Kyle asked from the bathroom.

"Well, I was going to try and go back to sleep, but that was before I knew you were awake," Jon said. "I hadn't really given any thought to plans for the weekend. I guess that makes me a crappy host, huh?"

Kyle peeked out of the doorway and said, "Not at all. You were probably thinking that we'd just spend the whole weekend in bed, right?" Kyle snickered.

Jon blushed. "Well, not the *whole* weekend but at least part of it."

"Fair enough," Kyle said. "But fortunately for you, I tend to be a planner, so I did some research, and I have some ideas for both today and tomorrow."

"Awesome," Jon replied. "I love it when someone takes charge."

"Oh, really." Kyle leered at him. "I'll have to remember that for later."

Jon walked over to Kyle and kissed him. "Promises, promises," he said coyly. "But seriously, what do you think we should do today?"

"I was thinking that we could head to Old Town. Walk around and be all touristy and have some food and drinks. I heard of a great restaurant called the Church Street Café that I thought we could try."

"That sounds great," Jon said. "What about tomorrow?"

"Are you afraid of heights, by any chance?" Kyle asked.

"No, why?"

"We could take the tram up to Sandia Peak," Kyle said. "There's a restaurant up there called TEN 3 because it's ten thousand three hundred feet up. Since it's Valentine's Day tomorrow, I *might* have made a reservation for dinner." Kyle smiled shyly. "We haven't talked about Valentine's, and I know that it's a made-up holiday, but it is our first together, so I wanted to do something special."

Jon smiled brightly and leaned in to kiss Kyle again. "What did I ever do to deserve you?" He pondered. "That's so sweet, and I love the idea of going up there. Some of the folks who were at the conference got in a couple of days early and were talking about it. They went up and said it was amazing. Frankly, I kind of forgot about it, but now I'm excited to go with you tomorrow."

"Excellent," Kyle said, hugging Jon tightly. "Now we have our plans set. We should probably clean up and head downstairs for breakfast."

Jon looked at him, grinned, and said, "Maybe we could shower together to um, ya know, save water?"

"Ha! I don't think we'll actually save any water that way, but I do like how you think," said Kyle, grabbing Jon's hand and pulling him into the bathroom.

THEY EXITED the Lyft on the edge of Old Town and began to wander with no real goal in mind, occasionally ducking into a store to browse, perusing some of the local arts and crafts, and enjoying each other's company.

Kyle would occasionally pull out his phone and take a photo of something—a sign, a building, whatever seemed to strike his eye. Jon found it charming that he wanted to document his visit and their time together.

Eventually, they found Mary Fox Park and decided to take a break. Sitting on one of the park benches, Jon turned to Kyle. "I'm so happy that you agreed to come visit me here. If I'd been here alone, I probably would have gone back home yesterday as soon as the conference ended or this morning at the latest. And I wouldn't have had a chance to see any of the city."

"I'm glad too." Kyle looked around the park, eventually gazing at Jon. "As I told you, I'd never been here before, so getting to see you and this city was a no-brainer for me. However, I would have agreed even if it was somewhere I'd already been. I really just wanted to spend time with you. As far as I'm concerned, getting to see a bit of Albuquerque is just a bonus."

Jon sighed.

"Uh-oh," Kyle said. "That sigh sounded a bit ominous."

"Not really," Jon admitted. "I'm just wondering what happens next."

"What do you mean?" Kyle looked confused.

"We're seeing each other, right? But we live over two thousand miles apart. I don't exactly have the best record when it comes to relationships—not that I've had many. Dylan was my longest, and he and I only saw each other for a few months. I dated a couple of guys in the past but never for more than a few weeks. Nothing ever seemed to fit—well, it seemed that I never fit into what they wanted me to be—so I've spent most of my adult life alone, searching for someone but never really finding them." Jon paused, trying to think of how to continue.

"From the moment I met you, I felt something," Jon said, his voice serious. "You were different, better than anyone I'd met before. I guess what I'm saying is that I don't want to fuck this up."

"Hey, I get it," Kyle said, putting his hand on Jon's knee and squeezing gently. "Okay, maybe I've been in a few more relationships than you, but nothing's ever really worked out for me either. So in that regard, we have a lot in common." He smiled as if he were trying to put Jon's mind at ease. "And granted, I've never been in a long-distance relationship. But I know people who have. My dad and Rob, for instance. Until recently, Dad was in LA, and Rob lives in Massachusetts. They managed to make it work. We'll figure this out. We both want it, so that's gotta count for something, right?"

"I love your optimism," Jon said. "But I always feel like I'm not good enough, and one day you'll wise up and kick me to the curb."

"None of that, now." Kyle looked at him sternly. "I care about you, Jon Rivera. It might be too early to say the 'L' word, but I'm definitely falling for you, and I want to do everything I can to make this work."

"Thank you; I want this to work too. Some days I feel really good about us, but other times, I just doubt myself and life in general."

"Hey, you're a work in progress. We all are in some ways. I

don't mean to pry, but have you talked to your therapist about this?" Kyle's voice was quiet, but Jon could hear the concern there.

"Yeah, I have, but obviously it's something that we need to talk about even more," Jon confessed. "I'm sorry, I didn't mean to get all heavy here. We're supposed to be having fun."

"We're also supposed to be talking about us and figuring out how to make this work," Kyle replied. "Besides, I'm with you, so I am having fun." He glanced at his watch, then stood and pulled out his phone, tapping something on the screen. "Don't know about you, but I'm getting hungry. I've got the directions to Church Street Café. I'm ready for some delicious New Mexican food and margaritas—let's go."

Sunday, *February 14 – Albuquerque*

It wasn't even six thirty in the morning, but they were both awake.

Their hotel room featured a Keurig machine, so Jon was making coffee for both of them. Kyle was in bed, reading on his Kindle. Returning to bed, Jon handed Kyle a cup, got under the covers, and reached for his own e-reader on the nightstand.

Despite trying to be in vacation mode, they'd both woken up early and couldn't go back to sleep. After a little make-out session, they decided to relax for a bit before getting ready.

"There's a place around the corner I'd like to go to for breakfast today," Jon said. "It's called Baca Boys Cafe, and the food is amazing. A few of us ate there earlier in the week."

"Sweet," Kyle said, grabbing this phone. After a moment of typing, he turned to Jon. "I just pulled up the menu. Everything sounds good, but I think I'm gonna get the breakfast burrito with *carne adovada*."

"Oh yeah, I had that. It's delicious."

Kyle hummed in agreement, then returned to his book.

After a few minutes, he dropped the Kindle to his lap. "Great, now all I can think about is food. I can't concentrate on what I'm reading."

Jon chuckled. "So go get ready. By the time we're both done, it will be close to eight o'clock, when they open."

BREAKFAST WAS DELICIOUS. As they left the restaurant, they decided to walk for a while. Even though they both had desk jobs, they were pretty active—Jon went to the gym a few times a week, and Kyle had an elliptical machine in his condo, which he used religiously. They'd been eating quite well on the trip, so a bit of exercise would be a good thing that morning.

After about an hour of strolling around the neighborhood near the hotel, they settled into a couple of chairs in the lobby. It was late morning, but they weren't going to go to Sandia Peak until the middle of the afternoon, so they had some time to relax.

"What are you reading?" Jon queried, opening his Kindle.

"A cozy mystery about a bookseller and her dog in Colorado." Kyle looked at Jon and smiled. "My dad got me hooked. Apparently, his assistant Julie is to blame. Julie, Sam, Rob, and my dad now have a group chat going where they recommend books and authors to everyone. I joined right after Christmas, and it's been great. Of course, I'll never have time to read everything, but I'm hearing about some great books."

"Oh, can I get into that? I'm always looking for something new. I'm reading a series about these two guys who own a detective agency in Missouri. They're gay and have been friends forever, and now they're a couple. It gets a bit angsty at times, but the writing is first-rate."

"Definitely. I'll send you an invite to the chat, and you have to share the details about that series with the group. I'm definitely interested in reading it."

<hr>

A FEW HOURS LATER, they went up to their room to freshen up. It was a beautiful day, with cerulean skies and temperatures in the low fifties, but it would be cooler at the top, so they wore heavier jackets and packed scarves, hats, and gloves into Kyle's backpack.

As he packed, Kyle turned to Jon. "Leave it to you to think of everything."

"Well, I knew you'd be here for the weekend, so I thought we might be spending at least a little bit of time outdoors." Jon smirked. "I wanted to be ready for anything."

They had prepared as best they could. If it got too cold outdoors, they'd go into the gift shop or bar until it was time for their dinner reservation.

Once Kyle had known that his Valentine's Day plans

were a go, he'd gone online and purchased tram tickets for the two of them, so after the twenty-minute ride from the hotel to the Sandia Peak Tramway, they got in line for the next tram.

"I'm really excited about this," Kyle said. "I checked out their Instagram account, and it looks like the views will be spectacular from up there."

"I'm excited too. After a few folks talked about coming here last weekend, I was kind of sorry that I missed it. But it will be so much better to be here with you." Jon smiled shyly.

Once they boarded the tram, they were told it would be a fifteen-minute ride up to the top. As the tram began its ascent, folks turned to look out at the ever-changing views. Jon and Kyle joined them, oohing and aahing at the magnificent scenery and taking photos with their phones the entire way up.

It was noticeably cooler at the top, probably fifteen degrees or so, and they quickly donned their extra gear. They walked around for a bit, taking more photos of their surroundings and each other, including a selfie or two. Jon said it was to remember the day, but in his heart, he knew he'd never forget their first Valentine's Day together.

"I'm getting a bit chilly," Kyle said after a while. "We still have a few minutes before our reservation; why don't we check out the gift shop?"

"Perfect," Jon replied. "I don't want to turn into a Popsicle today."

"Don't worry," Kyle said, heat in his eyes. "I'll warm you up when we get back to the hotel."

They each bought a refrigerator magnet to commemorate their tram ride. "I actually collect magnets and try to pick one up whenever I travel," Kyle confessed. "Neil always comments on my fridge at home, saying that the extra weight of the magnets will cause it to crash through the floor someday."

"Oh, now you've got to send me a photo when you get home. This I've got to see." Jon laughed heartily.

"I will," replied Kyle, joining in the laughter.

SEATED at a table overlooking the mountainside and the lights of the city below, they ordered drinks, then looked over the menu.

"Want to share the wasabi-crusted tuna for an appetizer?" Jon asked.

"It's like you can read my mind," Kyle replied, grinning. "I'm thinking about the miso honey-glazed tiger shrimp for my main course. What about you?"

"I think I'll get the pappardelle with grilled shrimp."

"Mmm," Kyle hummed. "That sounds good. Wanna get some white wine to go with dinner?"

"Sure. Neither one of us is driving." Jon's eyes sparkled as he spoke.

Dinner was spectacular, and their waiter convinced them to order the Chocolate Lover's Mousse for Two, the Valentine's Day dessert special. It was piped into a heart-shaped ramekin and was decorated with dark chocolate hearts, fresh strawberries, and whipped cream. The dessert was delicious, and even though they split it, Jon said, "I'll be spending an extra day at the gym this week in payment for all the food I've eaten this weekend. But it was completely worth it."

"Oh my God," Kyle agreed. "I'm stuffed, but yes, totally worth it. And my elliptical is my new best friend when I get home."

CHAPTER 8

"Want you." Kyle panted. "Will you make love to me? Please, Jon."

They'd barely managed to shut their hotel room door before they were in each other's arms, kissing passionately. Kyle ground his hardening cock against Jon's leg and whimpered. He kissed Jon once again, then unbuttoned Jon's shirt and reached for his belt buckle.

"I need you in me tonight, Jon," he said urgently.

Jon leaned into Kyle and sucked on his bottom lip, moaning. Unzipping Kyle's pants, he reached in and lightly squeezed his rigid dick. "Whatever you want, baby," Jon uttered.

They quickly undressed each other and got onto the bed.

Kyle reached between them and grabbed both of their cocks in one hand and stroked them slowly. They kissed hungrily, their tongues battling for dominance. Kyle licked the roof of Jon's mouth, then sucked on his tongue.

"Need more," Jon whispered, and Kyle flipped around. With Jon on his back, Kyle straddled him so they were mouth to cock. He slowly licked Jon from root to tip, then pulled Jon's foreskin back and encircled the head of Jon's cock with his tongue.

Pulling off, Kyle licked Jon's shaft again, then took his entire dick down his throat, hollowing his cheeks and sucking him deep.

Jon moaned around Kyle's dick, then nuzzled his furry sac and licked behind Kyle's balls, breathing in his scent. He smelled of citrus body wash and a muskiness that was pure Kyle. Circling his pucker, Jon swiped his tongue across Kyle's hole, then dipped his tongue in.

After a few minutes, Jon said, "Gonna come if you keep that up."

Kyle pulled off Jon's cock. "Want you in me, babe." He moved around and grabbed a condom and a small bottle of lube from the nightstand drawer.

Jon took the lube and squirted some on his fingers. Kyle lay back and spread his legs, bending them at the knees. Jon fingered Kyle's ass, slowing inserting one finger, then another, stretching him as Kyle removed the wrapper from the condom and rolled it down Jon's dick. He added some lube, saying, "Ready now, Jon. Fuck me."

Jon lined up the head of his cock against Kyle's hole and breached him. He paused once the head was in, giving Kyle a moment to adjust. "More, baby." Kyle panted.

Jon slowly moved forward until his balls rested against Kyle's ass. "Are you okay?" he asked, concern in his eyes.

"Yeah, sweetie," Kyle said, "but I need you to move, Jon."

Jon began slow, short thrusts, then slowly sped up, pulling almost all the way out and then pushing back in. He adjusted the angle of his hips until he hit Kyle's prostate.

"Yes!" Kyle cried out.

As Jon continued to rock back and forth, he leaned down and took Kyle's mouth in a smoldering kiss. Reaching between them, he stroked Kyle's cock, sucking on his tongue.

Before long, Kyle broke the kiss. "Coming!" He panted. His ass tightened around Jon's dick when he came, and that was all Jon needed, filling the condom with his release.

Their movements slowed, and their kisses turned tender. Jon slipped out of Kyle and removed the condom, tying it, then wrapping it in some tissues he found on the bedside table.

"That was amazing," Kyle said when his breath was even again. "So fucking amazing."

He leaned over and kissed Jon once again, then got up and went into the bathroom. A few minutes later, he returned with a warm, wet washcloth and gently wiped Jon clean. Tossing the cloth through the bathroom door, he crawled back into bed, and they cuddled together. Soon they were both fast asleep.

MONDAY**, *February 15 – Albuquerque, New Mexico***

· · ·

"Can we go back to Baca Boys Cafe for breakfast this morning?" Kyle asked from the shower. They had a few hours before they needed to be at the airport, and Kyle wanted to spend every minute with Jon.

Jon had showered first and was standing at the sink, brushing his teeth. "Sure. We've got plenty of time, and the food was great," Jon agreed. "I'm having that breakfast burrito again."

"Me too," Kyle said, pulling back the shower curtain and staring at Jon's perfect ass.

"See something you like?" Jon teased.

"Absolutely." Kyle pulled a towel from the rack and began to dry off. "We're still taking a Lyft to the airport together, right?"

"Yeah. My flight leaves later than yours, but I'd rather go to the airport with you. We can hang out together for a little while at least."

They dressed, sneaking in a few kisses here and there. Once they were ready, they left the hotel and walked to the restaurant for their farewell breakfast.

"This weekend really flew by," Kyle said, sipping his coffee.

"It did," Jon agreed. "When do you think we'll be able to get together again?"

"I've been thinking about that. I've decided that I'll talk to my dad and Rob sometime in the next couple of weeks. I've put it off far too long, and that's not right. Who knows, maybe I'm blowing this way out of proportion, and my dad won't have an issue with it. And if he does, I'll deal with it."

"Okay. But we're still across the country from each other," Jon said.

"How would you feel about coming to visit me in DC? Maybe in April?"

"Hmmm, that could work. I can see about getting some time off. We could do another long weekend," Jon offered.

"Could you make it a week? If you could catch a flight out Friday night or Saturday morning, we'd have almost 11 days together," Kyle responded excitedly.

"Wow, you have given this some thought, haven't you?" Jon chuckled.

Kyle smiled. "I told you I was a planner, right? And it only makes sense if you're flying all that way ..."

"Okay, let me talk to my boss and see what I can do." Jon shook his head. "I really can't say no to you."

"Good. Mission accomplished."

CHAPTER 9

Tuesday, February 23 – Washington, DC

"Wanderlust Travel, this is Samantha. How may I help you?"

"Hey, Sam, it's Kyle. How are you doing?"

"Kyle! It's so great to hear your voice. I'm doing well, how are you?"

"Things are great. Um, I actually have a favor to ask you, and I hope I can convince you not to say anything to my dad or Rob."

Sam was Rob's best friend, and that was how Kyle knew Sam. Kyle's dad, Ben, had met Rob a year and a half ago on a Mediterranean cruise, and they had started seeing each other shortly after that. Ben and Rob were now living together in Massachusetts. Kyle thought back to meeting Jon for the first time at London's Heathrow Airport, when they had all flown to England for Christmas the past year. He remembered finding Jon quite handsome and thinking there was something intriguing about him, but he had never expected to be in a relationship with Jon. The thought made him smile broadly.

"Hmmm, that sounds a bit suspicious, Kyle. What's going on?"

"Well, I'm not sure if you noticed anything, but Jon and I kind of took an interest in each other when we were in England, and we've kept in touch since then. I convinced Jon to come visit me in DC in a couple of months, and I'm trying to come up with something that's a little romantic that we could do here."

"I'm really glad you brought this up, Kyle. I did notice something in England, but I wasn't sure if I was imagining it or not," Sam confessed. "It sounds like you don't want your dad to know about Jon just yet ... I'm not sure how I feel about that."

"You're right, Sam. I do plan on telling Dad and Rob, but I've been a bit hesitant for a couple of reasons. One, I wanted to make sure that this thing between Jon and me is real, and two, I'm afraid that my dad may be a bit concerned about the age difference between us, so I'm slowly working up my courage." Kyle chuckled nervously. "In fact, I spent the weekend with Jon in Albuquerque a little over a week ago, and I can now say that things are going really well between us. But I need a bit more time to figure out exactly how I'm gonna tell them. I promise I'll do it soon and deal with whatever my dad has to say about it."

"First of all, I'm glad that things are going well with you and Jon. He's a great guy and hasn't had a lot of luck meeting good people. It looks like that's finally changed for him. Sure, I can give you some time. But I have to tell you that when I suspected something at the Mews, I did say something to Rob about my suspicions. I know he won't say anything to your dad, but I wanted you to know that I shared my thoughts with him. And between you and me, he doesn't have a problem with it."

"Whew, well, that's a bit of comfort, I guess. He could help my dad deal with it when the time comes." Kyle paused for a moment, then went on. "Thanks for agreeing to give me some time, Sam. I appreciate it."

"No worries, Kyle. If your dad asks me anything outright, I won't lie—but I will give you a heads-up if I end up telling him anything."

"That's fine, Sam. I really do appreciate your discretion. Now on to happier things," Kyle said, changing the subject. "Do you have any ideas about something Jon and I could do when he comes to visit? He said that he's been to DC before, so I don't necessarily want to do all the touristy things although we may do a few. I'd like something a bit romantic and kind of low-key. Jon's seemed a bit stressed lately, and I'm hoping that he'll be able to relax a little."

"Actually, I do have a couple of ideas, but I need to check on some things to see if the dates will work. When will Jon be in DC?"

Kyle gave her the dates, then said, "And while I'm not as well-off as my dad and Rob, I'm not overly concerned about the cost. I've still got quite a bit of the trust fund that my grandparents left me, and I'm doing well where I work, so I haven't had to use much of it recently. I can afford to splurge a little."

"That's good to know. One of the things I'm thinking of might be a tad pricey, but let me see what I can do. I'll call or text you with some info as soon as I can, okay?"

"That's great, Sam. Thanks so much for your help."

"No problem, Kyle. I'll talk to you soon."

They hung up, and Kyle breathed a sigh of relief. He'd been stressing about what to do during Jon's visit, but now that he'd talked to Sam, he knew she'd come up with some great options, and that assurance calmed him.

KYLE'S PHONE BUZZED, and he saw that it was a text from Sam. It had been a few hours since he'd called her, and he hoped that she had some good news for him. He opened the Messages app and read her text:

> I found something that I think you'll like. Can you call me to discuss details?

Kyle quickly texted back:

> At work now, but I can call you back in about an hour. Is that okay?

Sam's reply was a thumbs-up emoji.

KYLE WAS OPENING the door to his condo when he realized that he had never called Sam back. The afternoon at work had gotten crazy, and Kyle had gotten pulled into two different meetings. As a result, he'd completely lost track of time.

Grabbing a bottle of water from the fridge, he sat in his living room and called Sam's cell, figuring she might be home by that point.

"Hi, Kyle."

"Hey, Sam. Sorry it took me this long to call you back. This afternoon was insane."

"Not a problem. I totally understand. So, how would like to spend four days on a cruise along the Potomac?"

"What? I've never heard of cruises on the river," Kyle replied. "Tell me more."

"This is something brand-new and kind of an experiment. You know Ocean Cruises? That's the line that your dad and Rob spent a week on. They've started up a couple of river cruises in Europe but also decided to experiment with something in the US. Another cruise line is doing river cruises on the Mississippi, and Ocean is taking a chance on the Potomac. Between DC and a few spots along the river, they've put together some four- and five-day cruises for folks that want to do something different but don't want to be away too long."

"That actually sounds amazing," Kyle said. "But how much is this going to set me back?"

"That's the best part," Sam replied. "I spoke to a friend I have at the cruise line, and because they're in a testing phase of sorts for this, I was able to hold a stateroom on a four-night sailing for a really great price."

She relayed an amount to Kyle, and he exclaimed, "Oh my God, really? That's amazing. I'll take it."

"Excellent. I'll finalize everything for you tomorrow morning. I've got both Jon's and your info from when I booked the flights for Christmas. I've got high hopes for this little experiment by Ocean Cruises, so I'm sure you'll have a great time."

"Do you need my credit card number, Sam?" Kyle asked.

"Oh, that's right, your dad bought your flight in December, right?"

"Yeah, he did. Let me give it to you now and feel free to keep it on file just in case I need your help in the future."

"Fair enough, Kyle," Sam said, chuckling. "I'm ready for your card info."

CHAPTER 10

Wednesday, February 24 – Phoenix, Arizona

Jon had finished dinner and was sitting in his living room, flipping through channels on TV. He was feeling restless and thinking about calling Kyle; work had been crazy since he got back from Albuquerque, and he and Kyle had only managed to talk a few times. He was just about to start a video chat when the screen on his iPad lit up, displaying a FaceTime call from Kyle.

"Hey, babe," Jon answered the call, smiling. "I was just about to call you."

"Great minds and all that," Kyle replied. "How are you doing? You look tired."

"I'm okay, but work's been a beast lately. I am really beat. But I'm really glad you called. Needed to see your face."

"I wanted to see you too," Kyle shared. "I really miss you. I also have some news."

"Oh?" Jon replied, curious. "Good news or bad news?"

"Definitely good. Since you were able to get the time off in April to come visit, I called Sam yesterday to see if she had any ideas for something special we could do."

"You know you didn't have to go to any trouble, sweetie. I would have been fine just hanging out with you at your condo," Jon said.

"I know, but I really do want to do something special," Kyle answered. "Anyway, we're going on a four-night river cruise on the Potomac!"

"Oh my God, really? That sounds amazing. But wait, does that mean that Sam knows about us?"

"Hmm, yeah. But she promised she wouldn't say anything until I spoke to my dad. I do trust her," Kyle added. "And for what it's worth, she told me that she suspected something when we were all in England."

"Really? I guess we weren't as discreet as we thought," Jon replied.

"I know, right? But it's fine. I'm gonna call my dad in the next few days and see if I can visit him and Rob—I'm thinking about the first weekend in March—and I'll tell them what's going on, and then we can move forward."

Jon glanced down at the notepad at his side. "By the way, I started looking at flights to DC. Because of the two-hour time difference, if I leave in the morning, I won't get in until the middle of the afternoon, and I hate to lose most of that Saturday flying. But there's a red-eye Friday night that arrives at seven thirty Saturday morning. I can sleep on the flight, but I wanted to make sure that wasn't too early for me to get in. Of course, by the time I get my luggage and find a cab, it will be a more reasonable hour when I reach your condo."

"That's not too early at all," Kyle said. "And I'll either grab a Lyft or take the Metro and meet you at the airport. No arguments. I don't wanna waste a minute of the time I get to spend with you."

Jon laughed, his eyes sparkling. "Okay. No arguments from me. I'll book my flight tomorrow and send you the details." He yawned. "Sorry, it's not the company, I promise."

"No worries, sweetie," Kyle said. "I can tell you're exhausted. I'm gonna let you go so you can get some sleep, and we'll talk again soon. Sleep well, Jon."

"Thanks, babe. I'll call you before the weekend. G'night."

THE NEXT DAY

JON WAS SITTING at his desk sipping his morning coffee when Teresa walked in.

"Morning, Jon," she said cheerfully. "How are you doing today?"

"Good, T. How about you?" Teresa had been out for a few days entertaining her brother and sister-in-law who had come to visit, so Jon hadn't seen her in almost a week.

"Exhausted. As great as it was seeing Bill and his wife, I'm glad their visit is over. Trying to entertain them all the time took a lot out of me."

"They're heading up to Flagstaff now, right?" Jon asked.

"Yeah, they're planning on stopping in Sedona too. Not to

change the subject, but I'm kinda done with family right now. How are things going with Kyle?"

"Really good. We chatted for a little while last night until I started yawning. It's been really busy while you were away, and I'm really glad you're back." Jon drank more coffee and scratched his chin. "Kyle's planning on talking to his dad about us next week."

"Good. I know it's been tough on both of you, trying to keep the lid on that. So I guess this means it's getting pretty serious between the two of you?" She smiled, but there appeared to be a hint of sadness there.

"Yeah, the weekend in New Mexico seemed to solidify that for us," Jon confirmed. "But hey, why do you look sad about it? Do you think I'm doing the wrong thing by getting involved with him?"

"No, Jon, not at all," Teresa replied. "It's just that you probably won't have as much time for me anymore now that you've got your hot boyfriend."

"None of that. You're still my best friend, and I don't see that changing." Jon was concerned. They'd need to talk about this later.

"You're right, I'm just feeling a bit out of sorts after all that family time." She shook her shoulders as if to dispel her sadness. "Now, tell me what's been going on around here, and let me see if I can lighten your burden a bit."

CHAPTER 11

"Hey, Dad," Kyle said cheerfully when his dad's face appeared on his iPad screen. "How's it going?"

"Kyle!" Ben was sitting at the kitchen island in the home he now shared with his fiancé, Rob. He sipped from his cup and said, "I'm doing well, thanks. How are you?"

"Doing good. I was wondering if you and Rob were gonna be home this coming weekend. I was thinking of coming up for a quick visit."

"Is everything really okay, son?" Ben asked, the concern clear in his voice.

"Can't a son just want to visit his dad and his dad's future husband?" Kyle tried to joke about it, but it fell a bit flat.

"Really, Dad, I'm fine. But I do have something I want to talk to you about. It's nothing bad, but I wanted to do it in person."

"Of course, Kyle. And yeah, we'll be around this weekend. When do you want to come up?"

"I'm gonna see if I can get a flight Friday night. If that doesn't work, then Saturday morning for sure. And I'll fly back to DC on Sunday afternoon."

"Okay. Do you want me to call Sam and see if she can find flights for you?" Ben asked.

"Thanks, but I've got this." Kyle knew his dad had offered so that he could tell Sam to charge his card for Kyle's flights. Kyle appreciated the gesture, but it wasn't necessary. "I'm actually looking at flights right now. If I can't find anything in the next few minutes, I'll call Sam myself."

"Fine, Kyle. Send me your flight schedule, and I'll pick you up at the airport."

"Thanks, Dad. I will. Okay, I won't keep you. Say hi to Rob, and I'll see you both soon. Love you, Dad."

"Love you too, son."

***

FRIDAY, *March 5 – Westport, Massachusetts

THE HOUR-LONG FLIGHT WAS, as always, uneventful. Kyle's flight back home was less than forty-eight hours away, so he hadn't checked a bag—a small duffel and his backpack were all he needed. He quickly texted his dad as he walked from the gate at T.F. Green International Airport in Rhode Island. Yes, his dad and Rob lived in Massachusetts, but this airport was closer to their home than Boston's Logan International.

The ride to Rob and Ben's home in Westport was drama free, thankfully. It seemed as though his dad deliberately avoided asking what Kyle wanted to talk with him about, and that was fine with Kyle. Instead, they talked about Kyle's work, his friend Neil, whom Ben knew and Rob had met about eight months earlier, and Ben's brother, Mike, who was a lawyer in DC.

"Kyle, can I get you something to eat or a beverage perhaps?" Rob said when they entered the kitchen.

"Something to drink would be great, thanks," Kyle replied.

"I think I'll have some bourbon on the rocks," Ben added. "What would you like, son?"

"That sounds good, Dad. I'll have the same." Ben moved to the bar setup to make their drinks.

"Well, I'll let you two chat." Rob headed toward the stairs. "Your room is ready, Kyle. Make yourself at home."

"No, wait, Rob," Kyle called out to him. "I want you to be part of this conversation too."

"Okay. Ben, I think I'll have a bourbon as well, please."

Once the drinks were handed out and they were sitting comfortably in the family room just off the kitchen, Ben looked at his son and smiled. "So, what's going on, Kyle?"

Kyle sipped his drink and breathed slowly. *Better to just get it out there.* "I'm seeing someone. Um, for a few months now."

"Okay. But I suspect there's more to it; otherwise, that's something you could have told us on the phone, son."

"Well, actually, it's just that he—"

"Kyle, you honestly don't think I'd have a problem with you dating a guy, do you?" Ben asked.

Rob reached over and grabbed Ben's hand. "Just let him tell us in his own way, love."

"No, Dad, I know that wouldn't be an issue. I remember when I was in high school, and you told me that you were bi. I always figured it was your way of letting me know that it didn't matter who I dated." Kyle smiled at Ben.

"Not as subtle as I thought I was, huh?" Ben chuckled.

"I love you, Dad, and I appreciate the fact that you've always supported me. To be frank, I guess I'm bi too. I mean … I've dated both guys and girls in the past, but I guess I've always felt more connected to guys. But honestly, I've never felt really strongly about anyone. Until now." Kyle paused, collecting his thoughts. "The fact is, you know this person that I'm seeing."

It's not Neil, is it?" Ben asked. "I've always sensed that there might be something between the two of you."

"No, Dad, it's not Neil. Yes, Neil is gay, and we actually tried to date once, but we realized we were better as friends than as lovers. Neil's like a brother to me, so no. Nothing between us. It's Jon. The person I've been seeing is Jon."

Ben and Rob began to speak simultaneously.

"Jon wh—" Ben began.

"Wait, Sam's cousin?" Rob said.

"Yeah, her cousin. Jon Rivera." Kyle breathed out loudly and quickly grabbed his glass to have another sip of liquor.

"He seemed like a really nice guy when we met him at Christmas," Ben commented. "But isn't he a bit old for you?"

"This is exactly why I was afraid to say something," Kyle said, trying to keep his composure. "And why I wanted to do it in person. The age thing doesn't matter to me. Yeah, he's older, but we really connected over the holidays, and we've been in touch regularly since Christmas. In fact, Jon went to a conference in Albuquerque several weeks ago, and I met him out there for the weekend. We had a really good time together, and I asked him to visit me for a week in DC next month."

"Okay, son. I'm happy that you've found someone. But—" Kyle groaned when his dad said the word 'but.'

"Wait, let me finish," Ben continued. "I want you to really think seriously about this. Jon's what, about ten or twelve years older than you? I just don't want you to regret your decision later."

"Kyle." Rob looked at him. "You said earlier that you've never felt strongly about anyone until now. If you don't mind my asking, how exactly do you feel about Jon?"

Kyle's eyes lit up. "He's amazing. We 'get' each other, ya know? It's never felt uncomfortable when we're together. We can talk about pretty much anything, but even when we're not talking, it feels good. It feels right." Kyle sipped his drink again. "I know it's still early, but I think he might be the one."

"Hmmm, that kind of sounds familiar, doesn't it, Ben?" Rob asked, chuckling. "I distinctly remember someone flying to Florida to give me a red rose when Sam and I got to the hotel after the cruise and saying, 'Fuck anyone who says it's too soon.'"

"Um, yeah." Ben blushed, and Kyle laughed.

"You never told me that part of the story, Dad. You really did that, huh?"

Ben nodded shyly. "Guilty as charged."

"The heart knows what the heart knows," Rob continued. "If Jon were a stranger to us, I might recommend a little more caution, but hell, it's Sam's cousin. I can't imagine that she would have brought him into our family celebration if he wasn't a decent guy. Family or not."

"You're right," Ben said. "Thanks for reminding me of all that, love." He leaned into Rob and kissed him lightly. "And Kyle," he added, "I'm sorry if I wasn't as positive as I should have been when you first told us."

"Actually, Dad, this went so much better than I pictured it in my head." He grinned. "I might have had visions of you yelling and screaming."

Ben winced. "Damn, I'm glad I didn't do any of that. And I'm glad I have people in my life to call bullshit when I need it." He squeezed Rob's hand.

Rob sipped the last of his bourbon and stood up. "Refill, anyone?"

THE NEXT MORNING

"COFFEE?" Rob asked as Kyle walked into the kitchen.

"Please." He took the cup that Rob handed him.

"How did you sleep?" Rob drank from his own cup and sat at the island.

"Really well, thanks. I guess no longer having the stress of needing to tell you guys helped a lot." Kyle chuckled. "I might have overthought it all a little. And thank you for saying what you did last night. I believe it went a long way toward helping Dad absorb it all more quickly."

"Of course," Rob replied. "I do think your dad would have gotten there eventually, but I'm glad I could speed up the process for him. And I really hope that this all works out for you and Jon."

A timer dinged, and Rob pulled a muffin pan out of the oven. "Blueberry streusel," he announced as he set the pan on a trivet. "They need a few minutes to cool, but your dad should be downstairs once he gets a whiff of these, and then we can eat."

"Sounds good," Kyle replied, inhaling the delicious aroma of the muffins. "Do you know if Sam is around this weekend? I'd love to see her if she is."

"As far as I know, she's in town. I don't think she was going into the office this morning, but I'll call her cell in a little while and check. I'll ask her to come by this afternoon, and maybe we can all have dinner together tonight."

Ben entered the kitchen, sniffing. "Do I smell blueberry streusel muffins?" He kissed Rob and got himself a cup of coffee. "You need to visit more often, son. Rob doesn't bake these nearly enough." He laughed.

"Then we'd have to exercise twice as hard as we do." Rob lightly slapped Ben's hand as he tried to reach for a muffin. "They need to cool for a few more minutes."

"Rob's gonna see if Sam's around and ask her to come over today," Kyle began, changing the subject. "I wanted you both to know that she kind of knows about me and Jon."

"Wait, what?" asked Ben. "How exactly did Sam find out about your boyfriend before we did?"

"Relax, Dad," Kyle replied. "I've been trying to figure out how to tell you for a while. But as I explained yesterday, I thought you'd react badly, so I put off telling you for a bit."

"Okay, I get that, son, but you told Sam?"

"Well, when Jon agreed to come visit me, I called Sam to

ask if she had any ideas about something romantic we could do in DC. I might live there, but I don't normally have romantic adventures in town, so I needed some help. I had to tell Sam what was going on, and she told me that she suspected something when we were all staying at the Mews for Christmas."

"Sh-she what?" Ben stammered. He turned toward Rob. "Did you know any of this?"

"Calm down, sweetheart. Your blood pressure is gonna go through the roof," Rob responded gently. "Sam said that she suspected something, but it wasn't our place to approach Jon or Kyle. They're both adults, and it was none of our business if something were going on. And I certainly wasn't gonna say anything to you at that point. If Sam was wrong, that would only have made the situation worse. Not to mention really uncomfortable."

Ben shook his head and stared off into space, not looking at either Rob or Kyle. He seemed to be trying to slow his breathing. After a few minutes, he took another deep breath, exhaling slowly as he turned to Kyle. "Okay, I get it. It makes sense that Sam found out first."

Looking at Rob, he continued, "And I understand why you couldn't say anything sooner since no one really knew what, if anything, was going on."

Ben paused to sip his coffee. "I am feeling a bit blindsided, but after thinking about it, it's okay. Whew, it's just a lot to take in."

"I'm sorry, Dad. I probably could have handled all of this better," Kyle confessed. "I should know by now that I can talk to you about anything, but my brain went haywire, and I let it. For what it's worth, Sam did say that while she'd try to keep my confidence until I told you, she wouldn't lie if you asked her anything specific."

"It's okay, Kyle. I'm not crazy about how this all played out, but I do understand your thought process. I'm just happy that it's all out in the open now," Ben acknowledged.

"Thanks, Dad. And I do feel I need to apologize to Sam for putting her in the position of keeping things from you. I shouldn't have done that."

"Sweetie." Ben gazed at Rob. "Have those muffins cooled enough now? I don't know about you, but I've certainly worked up an appetite."

"Sure," Rob said as he passed out plates and refilled their coffees.

KYLE WAS in the family room, reading on his Kindle. Just after three thirty in the afternoon, Sam rang the back doorbell and walked into the kitchen. At first, Kyle was surprised, but then he remembered that Rob and Sam had been friends for a long time, and she was obviously used to just coming in.

"Hey, Sam!" Kyle said, getting up from the chair to greet her. "How are you?"

"I'm doing well, handsome," she replied, hugging him tightly. "How are things going with you and Jon?" she whispered.

"Really good, Sam. And no need to whisper. I told Dad and Rob last night."

"Ah, so that's the reason for this little visit." She winked and smiled. "I was surprised when Rob told me that you were here. How did that go?"

"Overall, it went well," Ben said, entering the family room with Rob. "Well, once I got over the initial shock, and Rob and Kyle managed to calm me down," he added with a chuckle.

They both hugged Sam. "And you've known for a while, you rascal, you." Ben tried to glare at her, but Kyle could tell there was no heat in his words.

"Sorry about that, guys. Kyle's family too, so I wanted to keep his confidence. But I did warn him that I wouldn't lie if either of you asked me outright."

"Yeah, he explained that," Rob said. "It's all water under the bridge at this point. We're all fine with what's going on."

"Good," Sam declared. "Now, one of you get me a drink, please, 'cause I've had a hell of a morning. I made the mistake of going into the office and got tied up in all sorts of things. I just should have stayed home."

"Wine, vodka, bourbon, something else? What's your pleasure?" Ben asked.

"Do you have the makings for an Aperol Spritz?"

"Of course, Sam. Anyone else?" Ben glanced at Rob and Kyle.

"Sounds good to me," Kyle replied, nodding.

"Yeah, I'll have one too," Rob said.

"Okay, Aperol Spritzes all around. Get comfortable and I'll have them ready in a minute."

"So, Sam," Rob began, "Kyle mentioned that he asked you for ideas on something romantic to do in DC when Jon visits him next month, but he never gave us any more details. What did you come up with?"

Sam grinned. "Oh my God, it's the best," she practically squealed. "Ocean Cruises is testing out a new river concept. It's already being done on the Mississippi, so they decided to give the Potomac a try. I was able to get a stateroom for a four-night cruise for a steal since it's still considered a trial run for them."

"That sounds great," Ben said as he passed out the beverages. "But there's not much to do on the Potomac, is there?"

"It doesn't go very far, but it will make a couple of stops along the river, and it even ventures out into Chesapeake Bay for a bit," Sam continued. "Just a nice little getaway that's meant to be more relaxing than anything else. Obviously, the ship is much smaller than a regular cruise ship, but it's also designed differently than a normal river ship that you'd see in Europe. I've seen some photos and a brief video, and it really looks great."

"You said they were testing this out, right, Sam?" Rob asked. "Any idea if it will continue?"

"I really don't know. They've invested quite a bit of money into this project, so I hope it does well. If it doesn't pan out, they could move the ship to the Mississippi. Only time will tell."

"Well, if they move to regular sailings, let us know. Ben and I would be interested in trying something like that, right, love?" Rob looked at his fiancé.

"Definitely," Ben agreed. "We could visit Kyle and take a cruise all on the same trip. Sounds perfect to me."

CHAPTER 12

Saturday, April 17 – Washington, DC

Jon woke up as the plane made its final descent into Ronald Reagan Washington National Airport. He'd been a bit restless at the beginning of the flight, probably because he was so excited to finally be visiting Kyle. Once they had taken off, he had read for a little while and then slept on and off throughout the journey.

Once they were at the gate, Jon grabbed his backpack and followed the signs for baggage claim. On the way, he remembered to take his phone out of airplane mode and saw a text from Kyle:

> Waiting in baggage claim. C U soon.

He smiled and texted back:

Almost there.

Checking a monitor, he located the carousel for his flight and immediately saw Kyle, looking as handsome as ever.

"Hey, beautiful," he said, walking up to Kyle. "Come here often?"

Kyle grinned from ear to ear. "Only when I'm meeting a stunner like you." He leaned forward and kissed Jon on the lips, then hugged him soundly.

"I've missed you so much," Jon whispered into his ear.

"Missed you too," Kyle agreed.

As luggage started arriving, Jon turned to face the carousel and search for his bag. After a few minutes, he saw it and easily retrieved it. They proceeded out of the terminal as Kyle tapped on his phone to request a Lyft.

"It should be here in roughly fifteen minutes," he said. "How was your flight?"

"Fine," Jon replied. "I was so excited to be coming here that I wasn't sure if I'd be able to actually sleep. But I read for a while and managed to get some rest for a good part of the flight."

"Good. I was hoping you'd be able to sleep on the plane. We'll drop off your bag at my place, and then I thought we could go to a place nearby for breakfast. It's called Commissary."

"That sounds great. I had a bite to eat before the flight, but I'm really hungry now," Jon confessed.

"Oh, the Lyft is here," Kyle said, glancing at his phone. He looked around and spotted the vehicle.

"There," he pointed.

Traffic wasn't bad, and they reached Kyle's townhouse about twenty minutes later.

"Oh, this is beautiful," Jon said as he entered the condo. Kyle gave him the nickel tour, pointing out a guest room and bath, a laundry room, and an exercise room on the first level. The living room, kitchen, dining area, and a half bath were upstairs. Finally, the third floor held the master bedroom with an en suite and a spare room that Kyle had turned into an office.

"Thanks." Kyle looked around at his home. "I got lucky and was able to buy this several years ago before the housing market went crazy. Even then, I normally wouldn't have been able to afford a place like this, but my grandparents set up a trust for me when I was a kid, and I was able to use some of that when I found this place. I've still got a mortgage, but it's manageable."

Jon dropped his bag and backpack in Kyle's bedroom and turned to face him. He smiled tenderly and hugged Kyle, kissing him deeply. "I'm so glad to be here with you."

Kyle returned the kiss, then broke it off, saying, "I'm glad you're finally here. But before this gets too heated, let's get you something to eat. We'll both need our strength so we can make out later."

"I like the sound of that, sweetie. Now lead me to the food."

AFTER BREAKFAST, they took a leisurely walk back to Kyle's condo. It was sunny and slowly warming up. The fresh air felt good as they strolled.

"Wow, that food was amazing." Jon patted his flat stomach. "I don't normally eat that much, but it was so good."

"I'm sure we'll get plenty of exercise this week, so no worries, babe." They both chuckled.

"I know I said I slept on the flight, but I might just need a nap this afternoon." Jon winked devilishly.

"I think we can manage to work off some of those calories and take a little nap today," Kyle said. "In fact, some sleep is probably a really good idea. We're meeting Neil for dinner tonight, and I don't want you falling asleep in your soup." Kyle laughed.

"Okay, so that covers today. I know how much you like to plan." Jon turned to Kyle and smiled. "What's on the agenda for tomorrow?"

"You know me so well already," Kyle admitted. "I thought we'd be tourists and take a walk along the Mall and maybe visit one or two of the Smithsonian museums. That is ... if you're interested in something like that."

"That actually sounds great. I haven't been to DC in years, and I've always enjoyed visiting."

"Excellent. Neil may join us tomorrow. He was on the fence about it when I asked him last week," Kyle said. "I think he is afraid of being the third wheel and intruding on our time together. I told him it was fine, and we'd be alone together on the cruise anyway, so we'll see what happens."

"I hope he does decide to join us. I know he's your best friend, and I want to get to know him better," Jon stated. "And you're right, we will have plenty of time together this week."

They climbed the stairs to the third floor, and Kyle pushed Jon against the bedroom door, claiming his mouth in a sizzling kiss. "Want you so bad," he growled when he finally broke the kiss.

Jon sucked at Kyle's neck as he toed off his shoes and began to unbutton his shirt. "Will you ..." he stammered. "Will you fuck me, please?"

Kyle reached for Jon's belt, practically tearing it off. He quickly had the zipper of Jon's jeans down and reached into his boxers to palm his hardening member. Yanking Jon's jeans and underwear down together, Kyle dropped to his knees and lunged at Jon's stiff cock hungrily, taking him to the root. After several moments of ardent sucking, he stood and guided Jon to his bed and pushed him onto the mattress.

Kyle took his phone out of his pocket, tapped something on the screen, then put it on the nightstand.

Once they were both naked, Kyle straddled Jon and kissed him once again, frotting their dicks together. He moaned into Jon's mouth, sucking on his tongue. He couldn't get enough of the man.

Moving lower, he swirled his tongue around Jon's tiny brown nipples until they pebbled in response.

"So good," Jon grunted as Kyle continued his ministrations and lapped at the trail of dark hair leading to Jon's navel and below. Kyle loved the fact that Jon only did the merest bit of manscaping, relishing the feel of his coarse hair against his skin. He slipped his tongue under Jon's foreskin and circled the head of Jon's cock, slowly stroking his own dick as he kissed and licked down Jon's shaft until he reached his hirsute balls.

Taking one into his mouth, he laved it thoroughly, then

started in on the other. "Ungh." Jon panted. "Wanna suck you."

Kyle flipped around, giving Jon access to his rigid cock as he dove deeper behind Jon's balls.

Jon sucked greedily on the head of Kyle's dick. Bending his knees, he spread his legs wide as Kyle teased his tongue around Jon's furry hole.

Licking down Kyle's shaft, Jon ran his tongue around Kyle's balls, then moved along his taint. Kyle reached for the bottle of lube he'd placed on the nightstand and poured some on his fingers. He worked Jon's hole, slowly opening him up with first one finger, then another, and finally a third.

"Need you in me now," Jon panted. "Can't wait anymore."

Kyle reached for a condom and quickly rolled it down his aching cock. Adding some lube, he lined up the head of his dick with Jon's hole and pushed in slowly. He didn't want to hurt him.

Leaning in for a kiss, he continued to push into Jon's ass little by little. Once he was fully seated, he stopped moving and kissed Jon again. "Doing okay?"

"More than okay, but you need to start moving."

Kyle slowly pulled almost all the way out, then moved back in again. He repeated the slow movements, letting Jon get used to the fullness. As he began to pick up speed, he kissed Jon again and reached between them to stroke Jon's dick in time with his own thrusts. He alternated between slow and fast thrusts and strokes, bringing Jon close to the edge, then backing off.

Sweat beaded on Kyle's forehead and dripped onto Jon's hairy chest. He changed the angle of his hips and pegged Jon's prostate as he sped up once again.

"I'm close," Jon uttered, breathing heavily. "Gonna co—" His orgasm tore through him, cum painting both of their stomachs and Kyle's hand. Jon's ass tightened around him, and that was all Kyle needed. He came hard, his cock pulsing and filling the condom. His breathing eventually slowed, and he collapsed onto Jon, not caring about the cum fusing them together.

They stayed like that for a few minutes until Kyle moaned. "If I don't move now, I'm gonna fall asleep, and neither one of us will be happy when we wake up stuck to one another." He rose, padding into the bathroom to clean up. He returned with a warm washcloth and a small towel.

He carefully wiped the now drying cum from Jon's body and dried him tenderly. He tossed the cloth and towel on the floor near the side of the bed, and he and Jon slid under the covers. They spooned together and drifted off to sleep.

A BUZZER WAS GOING OFF, and Jon woke up, confused.

"Alarm," Kyle muttered, his head half buried in Jon's chest hair. "Set it before. Um, before we, um, got busy. You know, before." He turned and shut off the alarm, then went back to hugging Jon.

"What time is it?" Jon asked, smiling. He wasn't used to Kyle being so incoherent.

"Five." Kyle was apparently still trying to wake up and was having a bit of difficulty forming complete sentences. "Sorry, still not awake." He rubbed at his eyes.

"S'okay. You're cute when you're half asleep." Jon reached

down and pulled Kyle's face up by the chin. He kissed the tip of Kyle's nose.

They snuggled for a bit longer. Kyle was just starting to drift off again when Jon asked, "What time are we meeting Neil?"

"He'll be here around seven. I told him to come here for a drink before dinner. We have eight-o'clock reservations at Logan Tavern. It's about a ten-minute walk from here."

"We should probably get up and shower, right? Don't want him catching us like this."

"Yeah, I'd never hear the end of it." Kyle chuckled. They trudged into the bathroom, and Kyle turned on the shower.

CHAPTER 13

Sunday, April 18 – Washington, DC

Sun streamed into the bedroom as Jon and Kyle slowly woke up. Jon's bladder reminded him that he had to attend to business, but he stopped and parted the drapes as he walked by the large windows. The bright azure sky held promise that it would be a beautiful day.

Jon thought about the night before as he peed. He liked Neil and was looking forward to getting to know him better that afternoon.

Kyle was just getting out of bed as Jon walked back into the bedroom. "I'll go downstairs and get the coffee started," Kyle said. Jon knew that Kyle needed some time and a little caffeine to get going in the morning.

After a leisurely breakfast, Jon and Kyle went upstairs to shower. They were getting dressed when they heard the doorbell ring. Kyle was just about to head down when he heard Neil call out, "I hope you guys aren't still in bed."

Jon recalled Kyle telling him that he and Neil had exchanged keys years ago, so he wasn't surprised to hear him.

"No, we've been up for hours, smartass," Kyle said. "Just getting dressed. Help yourself to a cup of coffee; we'll be down in a minute."

A little while later, Jon walked into the living room and found Neil sitting on the sofa, sipping his coffee while he stared at his phone. "Hey, Neil. Kyle's almost ready."

"Hi, Jon," Neil replied. "Ready to play tourist for the day?"

"I am. I told Kyle that it's been too long since I was last in DC, and I love the Smithsonian museums. I'm looking forward to seeing some of the city again."

Kyle descended the stairs. "Are we ready to go?"

Neil rinsed his cup at the kitchen sink, and they left, enjoying the fresh air and sunshine as they ambled to the Farragut West Metro station for the short ride to the Smithsonian stop.

Exiting the Metro station, Jon's senses were flooded with memories of visiting there many years before on a school trip. The trees in bloom along the Mall, the Smithsonian Castle, the Washington Monument—it was all a bit overwhelming.

"Wow." He took it all in. "I remember this like it was yesterday." He took Kyle's hand and squeezed it. "Thanks for bringing me back here."

"Of course, Jon," Kyle said gently. "Now, where do you want to go first?"

"Air and Space, then Natural History, I think." Jon was having trouble containing his excitement.

After a little over an hour in the Air and Space Museum, they exited into the warm spring air, and Jon sighed. "That was amazing."

They strolled a bit, people-watching as they went—families with kids, a couple with a dog, friends tossing a Frisbee around. It invigorated them after being indoors for a while. After about fifteen minutes, Kyle turned to Jon. "Ready for Natural History?"

"Yeah. Then we can talk about getting something to eat, okay?" Jon was enjoying himself tremendously, but he was also starting to feel a bit hungry.

Jon oohed and aahed as he viewed the various exhibits, and even Kyle and Neil got caught up in his excitement. "I forgot how great these places are," Neil said as they walked past the triceratops skeleton. "We need to make a point of coming here more often, Kyle."

"You're right," Kyle agreed. "We're so used to it all being here, we just kind of take it for granted. I think the last time I was here was about a year ago when my dad and Rob came for a visit."

A few minutes later, Jon turned to both of them. "Okay, I've seen my fill. Unless there's something you wanna do, I'm ready to leave."

They were heading toward the exit when Jon glanced at the African elephant in the rotunda. He stopped and stared. "Shit." He grabbed Kyle's hand.

"What's wrong?" Kyle asked.

"Jon, is that you?" A blond man approached them. He was of average height, with pale blue eyes and an athletic build.

"Dylan? What are you doing here?" Jon sputtered. "Are you following me?"

"Don't flatter yourself, Jon," Dylan replied, disdain clear in his voice. "I'm here for the weekend with a friend. And I might ask you the same question. You never could get enough of me." He smirked.

"I think you're delusional, Dylan. I broke up with you, remember?" Jon turned to Kyle. "Sweetheart, this is my ex, Dylan." Turning back to face Dylan, he stated, "This is my boyfriend, Kyle. I'm here visiting him."

Dylan looked a bit taken aback by Jon's announcement. "Boyfriend? I, um, I didn't realize you were seeing anyone," he stammered, seeming at a loss for what to say. All of a sudden, a mischievous look ran across his face, and he smiled seductively at Jon. "Well, if it doesn't work out, you can always call me, hun. I might consider going out with you again."

Just then, an older man approached them. "Dylan, baby, what's going on here?"

Before Dylan had a chance to reply, Jon looked at him in disbelief. "Excuse me, did you just try to flirt with me in front of my boyfriend? And it seems that you're seeing this guy." Jon gestured with his thumb. "What the fuck is wrong with you?"

Dylan blushed and turned to his friend. "Nothing, Ray. Just an old friend from Phoenix. Let's go."

"Don't let him fool you, Ray," Jon said as the two walked away. "He's a manipulative son of a bitch. I'm happy I figured it out before it was too late."

It appeared that Dylan and Ray were arguing as they retreated, but Jon couldn't hear what they were saying. He looked down and noticed his hands were shaking. He clenched them into fists, willing them to stop.

"Are you okay?" Kyle was studying him, his concern obvious.

"Sorry about that, guys." He looked at both Kyle and Neil. "And yeah, I'm fine—or I will be soon enough, I just need a minute." Jon paused, trying to steady his breathing. "And Kyle, I'm really sorry I outted you like that, but seeing Dylan just got me riled up."

"Hey, it's okay, babe. And seeing as I am your boyfriend, and you're mine, it wasn't really outing me. You were just stating a fact." Kyle smiled tenderly.

It had felt so good to finally stand up to Dylan. He'd never had the guts to do that before, but spending time with Kyle had made him feel better about himself; he wouldn't let people like Dylan get the best of him anymore. Jon took a deep breath and said, "I don't know about the two of you, but I need a drink right about now."

⁂

NEIL TOOK out his phone and began typing and tapping while the three of them walked toward the Metro Green Line's Penn Quarter station. After a few minutes, Neil pocketed his phone and said, "I've got a reservation at the Fainting Goat on U Street."

"I really need to apologize for making a scene," Jon said. "That's really out of character for me."

"Hey, you've got nothing to apologize for." Kyle looked at him. "Your ex is obviously a dick, and he deserved that and more."

"Kyle's right," Neil added. "I probably would have made a much bigger scene."

"Thanks, guys. I've never really stood up to Dylan before, and oh my God, it felt fucking awesome. I think you're a good influence on me, Kyle."

"I'm glad." Kyle smiled at him. "You're a wonderful, caring man, and no one should treat you like Dylan tried to. Damn, that guy is smarmy. If I'd been in his company any longer, I'd need a shower."

Jon chuckled. "He really is. It's funny, I didn't notice it when we first met, but it got worse and worse over time. I'm glad I wised up."

They had to wait a few minutes for a train, but the ride wasn't too long. It was only a couple of blocks to the restaurant once they'd gotten off the Metro, but they were still early for their reservation. Fortunately, a couple of people were leaving the bar, so they were able to snag two seats in the corner. Kyle told Jon and Neil to take the seats, and he stood between them. When another seat opened up a few minutes later, Neil spoke to the hostess about just staying at the bar rather than moving to a table.

Trying to keep the conversation light, they chatted about neutral stuff like work, favorite movies, and music. Jon talked about his friend Teresa, giving Neil a chance to know him better.

With their second round of drinks, they looked over the menu and settled on a few of the bar pies—the restaurant's version of personal pizzas.

Their conversation remained upbeat, and when the pizzas arrived, they dug in, enjoying every bite.

CHAPTER 14

Monday, April 19 – Washington, DC

Kyle opened his eyes. Seeing Jon lying next to him, he smiled. Today they'd be getting on the Azure Odyssey, Ocean Cruises' first foray into US river cruising. He'd been excited about the trip since Sam had booked it for the two of them. His reasons were twofold: he'd cruised before, but from everything Sam had said about it, this would be an entirely different experience; and more importantly, he'd be with Jon. Sure, they'd spent time together in England back in December, and he'd gone out to New Mexico to hang out with him a couple of months before, but their relationship had deepened since then.

In Albuquerque, Kyle had hoped that things would move forward in a positive way for them, but he had still been concerned about Jon. Physically, they connected, but emotionally, Jon seemed to be unsure of himself. After hearing about Dylan and seeing him up close the day before, Kyle could understand some of Jon's trepidation. But Jon had definitely grown over the past few months. Kyle felt good about how things were working out between them. He knew he'd fallen hard for Jon, and now it seemed like the feeling was mutual. Neither one of them had uttered the 'L' word yet, but Kyle knew In his heart that it would happen soon.

Jon blinked a few times and opened his eyes. "G'morning, beautiful."

"Hey, handsome." Kyle leaned over for a kiss. They kept it soft and tender, neither of them rushing to do more than just hug and kiss.

"What time do we need to be at the pier?" Jon asked.

"Check-in starts at two o'clock. From what Sam told me, that's a bit later than most cruise lines, but there's only a couple of hundred people to check in, so it won't take them long."

"Oh, good," Jon said. "We'll need time to pack this morning."

"Yeah, but it's only for a few days, and according to the paperwork I have, it's all very casual, so packing shouldn't take too long." Kyle picked up his phone from the nightstand and opened an email. "They've set up a small dock facility at Gravelly Point. That's near the airport you flew into. Apparently, they've got a parking area at the airport and will have shuttles available to transport us to the dock. Oh, and there's an app to download that has check-in information and deck plans, things to do on the cruise. I'll send you a link."

"Thanks. I gotta pee, but I'll download the app over coffee." Jon swung his legs over the side of the bed and plodded into the bathroom. Kyle ogled his naked butt as Jon walked away.

AFTER BREAKFAST, Kyle and Jon both sat at the kitchen island and concentrated on their phones. They were going through the check-in process, entering the required information so that check in at the pier would be that much easier.

Kyle had just finished everything when his phone rang. He looked at Jon and smiled. "It's Sam."

"Hey, Sam," he answered. "You're on speaker."

"Hi, Kyle. I assume Jon is with you?"

"Yeah, he is."

"Hi, Sam," Jon chimed in.

"Hi, Jon. Are you guys ready for your cruise?"

"We are," Kyle said. "We were just doing the online check-in stuff."

"Oh, good. It really helps to have that all done before you get to the ship. I just wanted to make sure you were all set."

"Yeah, we're fine," Jon remarked. "We just have to pack a few things, and we'll be ready to leave."

"Okay, I won't keep you. Have a good time, guys. I want to hear all about it at the end of the week."

"We'll be sure to call you, Sam. And thanks for making this happen."

"Of course. Love you, guys. Bye."

"She is such a sweet person," Kyle observed.

"That she is. But don't get on her bad side." Jon laughed. "She can be ruthless."

"Oh yeah. Rob's made that pretty clear." Kyle joined in the

laughter. "Okay, what do you say we go upstairs, shower, and pack?"

"Sounds like a plan."

KYLE HAD EXPLAINED to the Lyft driver that they'd need to look for signs when they reached the airport, and sure enough, there were large signs pointing them to the parking and drop-off area for the Azure Odyssey. They were met by a cruise-line representative, who checked them off a list, directed them where to drop their luggage with an attendant, and pointed out the shuttle buses.

There were only a few seats left, so they didn't have to wait long before the driver moved out to transport them to the ship.

When they reached the pier, a staff member said, "Please proceed to the large blue-and-white tent for security and check-in."

They got in the security line, where their IDs were checked, and their carry-ons were scanned. There was also a metal detector that they had to walk through, similar to airport security. Cruise-line staff were available to direct them to the check-in line, and within a few minutes, they were strolling onto the ship.

It was unlike any cruise ship they'd ever seen. "Wow, this is certainly different looking," Kyle said. Jon had acknowledged that he'd never cruised before, but he hummed and nodded his agreement.

The ship was low and long—only four decks high. They entered on the lowest deck and found themselves in a tastefully decorated lobby area where staff was waiting to assist passengers in locating their staterooms.

Kyle pulled up the boarding pass in the app and showed it to one of the cruise-line personnel standing there.

"Welcome, gentlemen, I'm Madeline. I can show you to your stateroom." She motioned with her hand to a stairway tucked into the corner. They ascended the flight of stairs and she led them down the hall to their cabin.

"Your luggage will be delivered sometime in the next hour or two," she told them. "There's a small safe in the closet for your valuables and bottled water in the mini fridge in this cabinet." Madeline opened a door near the desk, revealing the refrigerator.

Kyle noticed a bottle of bubbly in a wine bucket as well as two glasses on a tiny table near the loveseat. "And here is a complimentary bottle of prosecco to start your journey with us."

"Thank you," Kyle said as she walked toward the door.

"The bar on deck one is open now, and a buffet is set up in the dining room. Normally, all of your meals are ordered from a menu, but for embarkation day we provide a buffet since passengers are arriving throughout the afternoon." Madeline paused and turned toward them both. "If you need anything at all, please dial zero on any phone or speak with someone at the reception desk downstairs. Enjoy your cruise."

Once the door closed, Kyle reached for Jon and kissed him tenderly. "Welcome to your home for the next four days."

"Thanks," Jon smiled. "I'm not sure what I was expecting, but aren't cabins normally a bit larger than this?"

"Yeah, you're right." Kyle looked around the room. The cabin was smaller than what he had expected as well, but it was beautifully appointed in tones of sand and ecru, with pops of navy and lime in the pillows and artwork. "I think it's because this ship is designed for river cruising—there are a lot fewer cabins on this type of ship. And we do have a balcony." He slid the doors open, and they stepped onto a small but serviceable balcony with two cushioned chairs and a small round table. "We can have coffee out here in the morning or a drink in the evening."

"That's true," Jon agreed. "In any case, I wasn't criticizing. The cabin is lovely, and it's large enough for the two of us since we like to snuggle anyway."

As they walked back into the stateroom, Jon hugged Kyle from behind, kissing his neck. "Thank you for this. I know I said that you didn't need to do something this elaborate, but I'm glad you did."

Kyle grinned. "I'm glad I did too. Now what do you say we take a quick tour of the ship and get a drink at the bar? We can open that prosecco later."

"I like the way you think, babe. Lead the way."

IT DIDN'T TAKE LONG to tour the Azure Odyssey. Leaving their cabin, they went up to the top deck. There were a couple of rows of chaise lounges where folks could lie in the sun, some tables and chairs toward the back of the ship, and a small bar. Since the bar wasn't open, they turned around and went downstairs.

They'd both looked over the deck plans before leaving Kyle's condo. Knowing there were just cabins on decks two and three, they descended all the way to deck one.

Moving toward the back of the ship, they passed the reception desk and saw the entrance to the dining room. They noticed several occupied tables and a beautiful buffet set up along one side. Crisp white linens and pale sage walls gave the room a bright, airy feel.

They could see all the way to the back of the ship, and Jon pointed out an outdoor dining area at the far end. "Maybe we can have breakfast out there tomorrow morning."

"Yeah, I'm sure we can."

A hostess approached them. "A table for two, gentlemen?"

"No thanks, we're just taking a little tour," Jon said to her. "We're heading to the bar next."

"No problem, sir. You'll find it through the reception area. There are some light snacks available at the bar if you decide that you'd like something."

"Thank you."

The lobby was getting a bit busy as more passengers were arriving. Kyle noticed a small library tucked into a corner opposite the stairs, and the entrance to the bar was just beyond that. It was probably the largest room on the ship, with a U-shaped bar in dark wood at one end and an assortment of tables, chairs, and sofas around the room, arranged in smaller seating groups. In one corner sat a baby grand piano.

Kyle noted both leather and fabric-upholstered furniture, giving the room a warm, inviting feel. Entire walls of windows on either side of the room kept everything bright and cheery. Additional seating was available outside at the very front of the ship, just past the bar.

They worked their way to the bar, nodding hello to some of the passengers seated throughout the room.

"What can I get you gentlemen?" A smiling bartender

greeted them as they sat at the corner of the mostly unoccupied bar.

"I'd like Woodford Reserve on the rocks, please,' Kyle said, noticing the bourbon bottle displayed on the back counter.

"I'll have the same," added Jon.

The bartender deftly poured a healthy amount over ice into two crystal rocks glasses and presented them with a flourish. "I'm Josh. May I ask your names, please?"

"I'm Kyle, and this is my boyfriend, Jon."

"Welcome aboard the Azure Odyssey. Please let me know if there's anything I can do for you." With a final smile, he left them with their drinks and moved down the bar to wait on some other guests.

CHAPTER 15

Tuesday, April 20 – On the Potomac

"What's on the agenda for today?" Jon asked, sipping his coffee. They were at a table near the railing in the outdoor seating area of the ship's dining room and had just finished breakfast. They'd enjoyed a delicious dinner the night before and had then sat in the bar area, sipping after-dinner drinks and listening to a very talented pianist playing a wide variety of music, from popular hits and show tunes to light classical and jazz. It had been a very pleasant and relaxing evening.

"I have to admit," Jon continued, "I really haven't paid much attention to the itinerary for this cruise."

"Right now, the ship is just taking its time sailing down the Potomac," answered Kyle. "Because the distances between things along the river aren't very far apart, we'll head toward Chesapeake Bay, turn around, and then head back up to Mount Vernon. There's a shore excursion that's included in the cruise for a tour of Washington's home and the surrounding grounds this afternoon. For as long as I've lived in DC, I'm ashamed to admit I've never been to Mount Vernon, so I already opted in for that tour. We can pick up our tickets at the front desk when we leave here."

"That sounds nice," Jon remarked. "But it seems weird that we're going down the river just to turn around again. That's not usually how it's done, is it?"

"No," Kyle replied. "I can understand why Sam said this was a test for the cruise line. We are doing a lot of back and forth up and down the river, but unless they wanted to head into the open waters of the Atlantic, they don't have any other option."

"Hmmm, makes sense, I guess. Okay, so Mount Vernon this afternoon; what about the rest of the week?" Jon asked.

"Tomorrow is what they call a sea day on a regular cruise, but my understanding is that it's just called river cruising on a ship like this. We'll meander around for the day. I'm not exactly sure where we'll be going, but it will be a nice day just to relax. We'll be in the Norfolk and Virginia Beach area on Thursday for most of the day, then travel back up the Potomac and get off the ship Friday morning."

"From how things went in New Mexico, I know you like to plan things out. Have you thought about what you want to do on Thursday?"

Kyle looked up at Jon and grinned. "Yeah, I do tend to plan, but I try to be flexible too."

"Oh, I didn't mean anything bad by what I said. I actually

love the way you take charge like that." Jon looked at Kyle with half-lidded eyes. "It's kind of a turn-on."

"It is?" Kyle blushed. "I'll have to remember that tonight. But in answer to your question, I've looked at some of the activities for Norfolk but haven't decided on anything. I thought we could go through the information tomorrow and pick something out together."

"I'd like that," Jon agreed.

They'd finished their breakfast, so they left the dining room and strolled into the reception area.

"Since we have some time this morning, I think I'll grab my Kindle and sit outside to read for a bit," Jon said as they walked.

"That's a really good idea. Did you want to go up to the top deck?"

"Sure."

"Okay," Kyle said as they headed to the stairs. "How about you go to the cabin and pick up both Kindles, and I'll find a place for us to sit upstairs?"

"Perfect." Jon kissed him when they reached the landing for deck two. "See you in a few minutes."

***

ONCE THEY HAD DOCKED at Riverside Park, Kyle and Jon disembarked the ship and took a shuttle for the short ride to George Washington's Mount Vernon. Their shore excursion included a short tour of the mansion plus plenty of time to walk around the grounds.

They spent a little while at the Ford Orientation Center getting their bearings on what was available and what they wanted to see during the time they had there. They both agreed on the mansion, some of the gardens, the family tomb, and if they had time, the distillery, which was two and a half miles away and required another shuttle ride.

The mansion tour was first since they had a specific time to be there, so they set off to wait in line for that. Fortunately, the tour of the main house was less than a half hour long, so they had plenty of time to see the rest of the things on their list as long as they kept an eye on the clock.

The mansion was nice, but they both agreed that the rooms weren't as large as they had expected. From the east front side, the house overlooked the Potomac, and the views were beautiful. They meandered through both the upper and lower gardens, which flanked the bowling green just across from the main house. They were both fascinated by the necessaries, or privies, located on either side of the green, however they both agreed that having to go outside to use the toilet wasn't their idea of a fun time.

At the last minute, they decided to skip the tomb and went back to the orientation center to catch a shuttle to the gristmill and distillery since they were both anxious to see that part of the property.

"This gristmill is gorgeous," Jon said, eyeing the building for the first time. It was a beautiful four-story stone building, and together with the millrace, Dogue Creek, the rustic wood rail fence, and the surrounding wooded area, it was very picturesque.

"I think this is the best part so far," Kyle agreed. "I need photos."

Between the distillery tour and the walking they did

around the mansion and gardens, they were both more than ready to return to the ship a few hours later.

By the time they got back to the ship, it was almost six o'clock. Jon consulted the ship's app once they were back in their cabin.

"The dining room is open until eight thirty tonight," he offered, slipping off his shoes. "How would you feel about taking a little nap before having dinner?"

"Oh my God, it's like you are reading my mind," Kyle said. "The tour wasn't overly strenuous or anything, but I think all the fresh air is getting to me. Why don't we nap for an hour, then clean up and go to dinner after that?"

"Perfect. I'll set an alarm on my phone."

They got under the comforter and gently slipped off to sleep.

Sipping drinks as they reviewed the menu, a martini for Kyle and bourbon on the rocks for Jon, they both decided on Caesar salad to start and the Chilean sea bass for their entrees.

After the waiter took their orders, Kyle said, "I'm so glad we took that little nap. It was exactly what I needed."

"Yeah," Jon agreed, smiling. "I do have a good idea every now and again."

"Oh, I think you have very good ideas pretty regularly," Kyle teased.

"I have a few ideas about what we might do later tonight,

seeing as how we got good and rested earlier." Jon's grin widened mischievously.

Just then the waiter approached with their entrees, ending their flirting.

The fish was served with an herbed lemon-butter sauce, parslied potatoes, and grilled green beans. It looked fantastic.

"May I get you anything else?" the server asked. "More drinks perhaps?"

"I'd like a glass of the Kim Crawford Sauvignon Blanc, please," Kyle answered.

"I'll have another bourbon, please," replied Jon.

The mood broken, their conversation turned to more mundane things.

Skipping dessert, they left the dining room and strolled around the ship for a little while. They stood at the rail outside of the bar area and enjoyed the gentle breeze as they sailed past Caledon State Park and Colonial Beach. The moon reflected on the river, and they could hear the lapping of the water as the ship drifted forward. Jon realized he'd never been as happy as he was at that very moment.

He reached for Kyle's hand. "I'm happier now than I've ever been before, Kyle, and that's mostly because of you. You've helped me in ways I couldn't imagine."

Kyle leaned in so their shoulders met. The heat from Kyle's arm felt so soothing, and Jon gasped in realization at what was happening between them.

"I haven't been with a lot of guys. In the few relationships —or almost relationships—I've had, the guys have been younger, and they all assumed because of my age that I was more experienced than I am. That usually led to misunderstandings. Or maybe I've just never met the right guy. Whatever the reason, I've often felt like a failure and that things never work out because of me. The older I get, the worse it has gotten."

Jon continued, "You're different, Kyle. I don't know how else to explain it, but you get me. You've never made me feel like I'm inadequate. I think for the first time in my life, I feel whole with you."

Kyle looked into Jon's eyes. "You don't realize how special you are, Jon," he said softly. "There's something about you that just melts my heart."

"Many might say it's too early to know, but I don't need any more time. I love you, Kyle."

"I love you too, Jon. I think at least part of me has since England. It's gonna sound so corny, but there's that movie where one of the characters says, 'You complete me.' I don't think I understood what that really meant until now."

They kissed. They were alone on the deck, so what started out quite tender heated up pretty quickly. Jon licked up Kyle's neck and nibbled on his ear. Kyle's hands ran down Jon's back. When he reached Jon's ass, he squeezed and pulled Jon close, feeling him harden and lengthen against his belly.

Moaning, they reluctantly pulled away. "We should take this somewhere more private." Kyle tried to adjust himself, knowing they'd likely meet others on their way back to their cabin.

"Yeah." Jon was breathless as he did the same.

THE LIGHTS WERE dim when they entered the stateroom, and they moved in unison as they slowly undressed each other.

The soft hiss of fabric moving against skin, the snick of zippers lowering, and soft moans and gasps filled the air.

When they were both nude, they fell onto the bed, hugging and slowly kissing. Things ramped up quickly, and Jon pleaded, "Take me, Kyle. Make me yours."

Kyle licked along Jon's Adam's apple, moving lower to suckle on a hard brown nipple. He moved on to the other, laving it thoroughly as Jon's coarse chest hair tickled his nose. He continued his southward journey, kissing down the trail of dark hair past Jon's navel. Planting a gentle kiss on the underside of Jon's cock, he moved further down and nuzzled the space between Jon's hairy balls and thigh, inhaling deeply. He smelled the cruise line's fragrant body wash and a spiciness that was all Jon. He knew he could get lost in that scent forever.

Kyle slowly licked first one ball, then the other, continuing up the rigid shaft. Pulling back the foreskin, he encircled the velvety head with his tongue. Lapping the pre-cum pooling at Jon's slit, Kyle took the head of Jon's cock into his mouth and sucked. Pulling off, he tickled Jon's frenulum with the tip of his tongue, then took him to the root.

"Oh God, please!" Jon panted. "So fucking good!"

Kyle reached behind Jon's knees and pulled both of his legs up. Jon quickly caught on and grasped his own legs, bringing his knees up to his chest, exposing his most private place. Kyle moved still lower, running his tongue through the wiry hair until he reached his prize.

Kissing Jon's pucker, he began licking and stroking his tongue back and forth across his hole. "Open up for me, babe."

Pointing his tongue, he plunged into Jon's hole over and over again.

"Yes! Please fuck me!" Jon cried out.

"Not 'til I get you ready, sweetie."

Kyle reached for the bottle of lube sitting on the nightstand and squirted some onto his fingers. He circled Jon's rim and slowly inserted one finger just enough to breach him. He moved slowly and patiently, eventually working his entire finger into Jon. He slowly stroked the spongy bundle of nerves, and Jon moaned. He would make this so good for Jon, he thought.

Kyle began to suck Jon's cock, working a second, then a third finger into him.

"I'm good, Kyle. I'm ready. Please, I need your cock in me now," Jon commanded.

Kyle heard the condom wrapper tear. Jon half sat up and rolled the rubber down Kyle's length and quickly rubbed some lube onto his shaft.

Lying back down, he stared into Kyle's eyes. "Now."

Kyle positioned the head of his cock at Jon's waiting hole and pushed. He watched as the head slipped in, then stopped, looking at Jon to make sure he was okay.

"More," Jon pleaded.

In one slow but steady stroke, Kyle moved forward until his balls rested against Jon's ass. He leaned forward and caught Jon's mouth in a scorching kiss.

And then he began to move.

Pulling almost all the way out until just the head of his dick remained inside Jon, he plunged back in. He moved slowly at first, but then the rhythm began to build. He moved faster and faster.

This feels right. Perfect. This is how it's supposed to be. Yes, this is what it feels like when you love the person you're making love to.

Despite the speed of their lovemaking, there was a calmness, a peace to it.

Their kiss deepened even further. Jon sucked on Kyle's tongue, matching the speed of Kyle's cock moving in his ass. The head of Kyle's cock caressed Jon's prostate, and Jon moaned into his mouth.

One of Jon's hands moved down Kyle's back until he reached his hole, slipping a finger inside.

Kyle took that cue to speed up just a bit. He sensed a quickening in Jon, then felt wetness as Jon splattered their bellies with his hot cum.

Jon's orgasm was all Kyle needed. As Jon's channel tightened around Kyle's cock, he came, filling the condom with his seed. After a few moments, he slowed his thrusts and breathed heavily.

"Oh my God!" Kyle cried.

"That was ..." Jon trailed off, his brain failing to supply the words.

"Yeah." Kyle tried to slip out of Jon, but Jon held on to his ass, keeping him in place.

"Please don't move. I love how you feel inside me. I feel whole when you're there."

They stayed together like that, slowly exchanging kisses until their breathing was almost back to normal.

"Love you, Kyle."

"Love you too, Jon."

After a few minutes, Kyle slowly pulled out of Jon's ass. "If we don't move, we're both gonna fall asleep and wake up stuck together. That won't be pretty."

Jon sighed, missing the fullness of Kyle inside him. "You're right."

Kyle padded to the bathroom, removing the condom and tying it off as he went. After cleaning himself up, he returned with a washcloth that he'd run under warm water. He tenderly cleaned Jon, then dried him with a hand towel.

He dropped the cloths over the side of the bed, then he and Jon both got under the covers. Kyle rested his head on Jon's chest and wrapped an arm across his stomach. Feeling sated and relaxed, they both fell into a deep sleep.

CHAPTER 16

Wednesday, April 21 – On the Potomac

They slept in.

Fortunately, Kyle had had the presence of mind to place the breakfast order form on the door handle the previous night, checking off the latest time possible: ten fifteen. A knock on the door woke him, and he allowed the waiter to place the tray containing a pot of coffee and continental breakfast for two on the small table in front of the loveseat.

The waiter departed, generous tip in hand, and Kyle crawled back under the duvet, snuggling up to Jon as he drifted off to sleep again.

When he woke the next time, Jon was staring at him, looking content. "Morning, sunshine."

"Hey, babe." Kyle leaned into him and kissed him soundly.

145

"What time is it? Breakfast got here earlier, but I fell back to sleep."

"It's just past eleven, and well, we did burn a few calories last night." The edges of Jon's mouth quirked up in the beginnings of a smile.

"We sure did," Kyle agreed. "And let's not forget round two around three fifteen this morning."

Kyle had woken up in the middle of the night with Jon nuzzling his neck, his hard cock pressed into Kyle's crease. That turned into more kissing and rubbing and tasting and well, let's just say they were both well fucked by morning.

"I need nourishment," Jon declared, rising and plodding to the bathroom. Kyle could hear him relieving himself and reluctantly got up to pour them each a cup of coffee; the carafe, thankfully, had kept it piping hot. Lifting the covers on the plates, he found an assortment of pastries and some artfully arranged fresh fruit.

Jon placed a towel across the loveseat, and they sat naked together and ate, feeding each other bits of croissant, mango, cheese Danish, and strawberries. It was delightful; Kyle couldn't help but smile.

"What did you want to do today?" Jon asked as they sipped the last of the coffee.

"You," Kyle teased.

Jon almost choked.

"Seriously, I just want to relax and spend time with you." Kyle smiled a tender and caring smile.

After a leisurely shower together, they dressed, grabbed their Kindles, and went for a stroll around the ship.

They'd read that the ship normally held just under one

hundred fifty passengers, but there were fewer on this sailing, so there was plenty of space to relax.

The ship was meandering along the coast near Chesapeake Bay, moving up toward Annapolis and down to Newport News, with no real destination in mind. This was to be a low-key day at sea; the passengers seemed content to just hang out and enjoy the ship and the scenery.

Kyle and Jon passed a few small groups in the bar, playing cards or chatting, but they decided to check out the upper deck and enjoy the sunshine and coastal breezes. They located a couple of lounge chairs toward the back and settled in with their e-books.

A little while later, a bar waiter approached. "May I get you anything from the bar?" he asked.

Kyle glanced at his watch, and seeing it was after one o'clock, ordered an Aperol Spritz.

"That sounds good. I'll have the same, please," Jon added.

They continued in relative silence for over an hour until Jon sighed and placed his Kindle on his lap.

"What's wrong, love?" Kyle reached for Jon's hand, squeezing lightly.

"I keep thinking 'What happens now?'. With us, I mean. I love you, and you love me, but we live over two thousand miles away from each other. Can we really make this work?" Kyle saw the sadness clearly etched on Jon's face and frowned slightly. He hated seeing Jon troubled. No, it wouldn't be easy, but if they worked at it, he knew they *could* make it happen.

"Um, that is to say, ah ..." Jon continued, stammering. "I mean, you want to make this work, right?" He sounded unsure of himself, and Kyle's heart cracked just a bit.

"Of course, I want to make us work, sweetheart. I meant it when I said I love you, and I believe we can figure it all out. It may take some time, and it might not be the easiest thing we've ever done, but we're in this together, and we can do it." Kyle spoke with conviction, maybe a bit more than he felt at the moment, but he needed to reassure Jon more than anything else. He was rewarded with a bright smile on Jon's face. It warmed his heart. *That bastard Dylan did so much damage to you,* he thought. *I'll do everything in my power to show you how wonderful you really are.*

Kyle could sense a certain amount of relief from Jon, but he also sensed something else lurking.

"Is that all that's bothering you, babe? You know I'm here for you, right?"

"Yeah, I do. And I can't fully express how much that means to me. Bernie's always had my back, and I know I always have T's support, but I didn't always feel that from the few guys I dated. Especially not from Dylan. I'm sorry if I sound needy or whiny, but I'm not used to my relationships working out, so I tend to be insecure." Jon paused for a moment. He seemed to be collecting his thoughts, so Kyle stayed silent.

"Plus, I'm still worried about my mom. Well, my mom and me. I told you we kind of came to a tentative understanding, but I'm not convinced it's gonna last. She's done this kind of thing before, and it always comes back to the fact that she expects me to give her grandkids. I just don't know if that's gonna happen. Again, just call me Mister Insecure." He smiled.

"Hey, it's okay. I'm sorry that you haven't had the most supportive boyfriends in the past, but that's changed now. You've got me, and I've got you." Kyle rubbed Jon's knee, trying to will his support into the man he cared so much for. "I know it's not easy ... but try not to dwell on it right now. Let me think about it for a while. I might be able to come up with an idea or two."

"Thank you, Kyle." Jon took Kyle's hand and brought it to his lips, kissing the knuckles tenderly.

Eventually, they made their way back to their cabin, and things got frisky.

Up until that point, they'd enjoyed being intimate with each other—when they were in Albuquerque, on a few video calls, and when Jon first got to DC. But in many ways, Kyle could see that they were still just testing the waters, and it had been more about having fun and enjoying each other. Declaring their love for each other had connected them on a whole new level. They couldn't get enough of each other.

Kyle pushed Jon onto the bed and quickly unzipped his fly, pulling out Jon's flaccid cock. He sucked him greedily, quickly working him to full arousal, licking and nibbling. He loved the feel of Jon's foreskin, gently tugging the edge and running his tongue between it and the head of Jon's dick.

"Come up here." Jon panted. "I want my mouth on you too."

Kyle shoved his pants and underwear off and straddled Jon's face, then went back to his ministrations to Jon's leaking cock.

Jon wasted no time burying his face in Kyle's ass. He laved his hole, then worked his tongue down along Kyle's fuzzy sac, licking and kissing along his rigid length. He sucked the head into his hot mouth, swirling his tongue around the crown, then took him all the way into his throat.

"Ungh!" Kyle cried out. Letting Jon's cock slip from his mouth, he croaked, "I'm close. So fucking close."

"Me too." Jon's voice was low and sultry.

"Ah!" Kyle came, and Jon immediately followed. They lapped at each other's release, slowly bringing each other down until their breathing normalized, and they were completely cleaned. After one more swipe of Jon's tongue along his ass, Kyle lifted and pivoted so that he faced Jon, lying halfway on top of him.

"Mmm," Kyle moaned. He kissed Jon, tasting himself as he sucked on Jon's tongue.

They slept.

When Kyle awoke, it was seven o'clock. Dressed in only his shirt and socks, he rose and picked up his pants and trunks off the floor.

He heard Jon stir. "What time is it?"

"It's just seven. We should shower and then go to dinner."

Jon grunted in what Kyle assumed was the affirmative. Although still fully clothed, his fly was open, and his dick was hanging out. They managed to quickly shed their clothes, then efficiently lathered each other and rinsed off.

Once dressed, they shared a single, tender kiss and left for dinner.

CHAPTER 17

Thursday, April 22 – On the Potomac

The ship was docked near Virginia Beach for most of the day, giving them access to Norfolk, Portsmouth, and Newport News.

"I think there are some brochures at the front desk." Kyle sipped his coffee. They were eating breakfast in the dining room, discussing what they might want to do that day. "I'm happy with keeping it low-key if that's okay with you."

"Definitely. I'm more interested in just hanging out with you although a walk might be nice." Jon dipped his head slightly and smiled shyly. That look always touched Kyle's heart. How he loved this man.

"Okay, once we're finished, let's check out our options."

They shared eggs, French toast, and bacon. As soon as they

had enjoyed one last cup of coffee, they set off for the main reception area.

As they entered the space, there were a few people milling about, and one of the ship's staff approached them.

"Is there something I can help you with?"

"We're trying to decide what to do today," Jon answered for them. "We're really not interested in sightseeing. Is there anywhere nearby where we could just go for a walk?"

"Yes, there are a few options for you." He pulled a folded map from a small rack at the desk and opened it. "We're here, docked near Grommet Island Park. Virginia Beach runs all the way up to First Landing State Park. It would take you about two hours to walk there, but we've got shuttle buses running back and forth, with a few stops along the way. Depending on how much exercise you want to get, you can take a shuttle there and walk back or just hike a bit at the park and take shuttles both ways."

He folded up the map again and handed it to Jon. "Take this. It will show you where the shuttle stops are along the way. The last shuttle leaves the main pickup point at the park at five thirty this afternoon."

"Thank you so much," Kyle said.

"No problem. And don't forget to pick up a couple of bottles of water when you leave the ship."

The day was sunny and warm, but Kyle thought it might be breezy at the beach, so they grabbed light jackets along with their Kindles and sunglasses. Kyle packed it all up in a small backpack he'd brought. Stopping for the requisite bottles of water on their way off the ship, they set off to get some fresh air and explore a bit.

They walked along the beach for a while, enjoying the sunshine and ocean breeze.

"This is wonderful," Jon said, taking Kyle's hand in his. "I'm having the best time."

"I'm glad," Kyle replied. "This has been fun for me too. I never take the time to do any tourist stuff here. And Sam really did a great job with this cruise. It's not typical, but having this little break in routine gave us a chance to do things I wouldn't have thought of."

"I agree. Although someday, I'd like to go on a regular cruise with you."

"I'm sure we can make that happen." Kyle nodded. "In fact, my dad and Rob have been talking about their wedding plans, and they're considering a honeymoon cruise with family and friends, so if you can get the time off, that's a possibility in the fall."

"Really?" Jon's expression showed surprise. "They want to bring people on their honeymoon with them?"

Kyle laughed. "I said the same thing to my dad. He explained that since this is a second marriage for both of them, they wanted to do something more inclusive for the people that mean a lot to them. Now, the cruise thing isn't set in stone, but I expect we'll hear more in the next couple of months."

A few minutes later, they reached a shuttle stop and decided to wait for the next bus to catch a ride to First Landing.

They arrived at the state park after a short twenty-minute ride along the water. They walked along the beach and ventured around the various facilities, taking photos when something caught their eye. They managed to take a few selfies too. After almost two hours of walking, with an occasional stop here and there, they waited in a short line for another shuttle back to the ship.

"Do you wanna get off a stop or two early and stroll a bit more, or have you had enough exercise?" Kyle asked as they took their seats on the shuttle.

"It feels good to be moving. Let's get off the shuttle before we reach the ship and walk the rest of the way back."

———

WHEN THEY GOT off the bus a few minutes later, Kyle turned to Jon. "So, I've been thinking about the situation with you and your mom, and I have an idea."

"Do tell," Jon said excitedly.

"I don't know if this will work, or if it's even feasible, but have you considered switching houses with Bernie?"

Jon stared at him, face blank, unblinking. Kyle thought he'd perhaps gone too far and was way off base with his suggestion. "Um, I dunno, like I said, it might not even be feas—"

In a flash, Jon's expression morphed into one of shock—or surprise. His eyes grew wide, and his jaw hung open.

"Whatever made you think of that?"

"I remembered you telling me that your mom is pushing for more grandchildren, and that she loves spending time with Bernie's kids. You said that you and Bernie don't live all that far away from each other, and I got to thinking that if your mom could spend more time with her existing grandkids, it might take some of the pressure off you."

Kyle paused, trying to decide if he should continue.

When Jon just continued to stare, he barreled on. "I don't even know if it's something that Bernie and her family would consider, but I figured it was at least worth mentioning."

"It's absolutely brilliant!" Jon exclaimed. "I'm sorry if I didn't react right away, but I was processing." He smiled. "I don't know if I ever told you this, but the only reason I got the house was because I was the male. It's a stupid, archaic way of doing things, but my parents wanted me to have the house so that I could take care of a family. When Bernadette got married, her husband was expected to provide for her.

"But it's not right. The house is way more than I need. In fact, I tried to give Bernie the house when she got married since she would be starting a family. But my parents wouldn't hear of it. I'll talk to Bernie, and if she and Jeff are okay with it, maybe we can talk my mom into it now."

"Well, I hope that this is at least the start of setting things right with your family." Kyle smiled, happy to try and help his man.

By that point, they'd reached the ship and decided to stop in the bar for a drink after all the exercise they'd gotten. Hopefully Josh, their favorite bartender, would be working.

***

THEY WERE SITTING in the dining room waiting for their entrees, a filet mignon for Jon and shrimp Mozambique for Kyle, when Kyle's phone buzzed.

Glancing at the screen, he looked up at Jon. "I meant to tell you about this when you first got to DC, but it completely slipped my mind. That was a text from my uncle Mike. I try to have dinner with him and my aunt Ellen once a month or so, and we're scheduled for tomorrow evening."

"Oh, that's no problem," Jon offered. "I can hang out at your place. I'll be fine."

"What? No, um, I mean, I'd like you to join us if that's okay. When I spoke to Uncle Mike last week, I mentioned that you'd be in town. You met them over Christmas, so you already know them, and now that you're my boyfriend, it makes sense that we'd go together, right?"

"Boyfriends. Yeah, I really like the sound of that." Jon reached for Kyle's hand. "I'd love to go to dinner with you and Mike and Ellen."

"Cool. Let me just text him that we're still on, then we can finalize plans tomorrow after we get back home."

Just then, their server arrived with their food. When they declined anything else, the waiter departed, and they dug into their delicious meals.

"Once again, the meal was amazing." Jon patted his belly, chuckling. "And I'm skipping dessert again tonight."

"I know what you mean," Kyle agreed. "Even though we've done our fair share of walking on this trip, I don't normally eat like this at home. Gonna have to work out a bit more next week."

Leaving the dining room, they used one of the outside doors and ambled along the deck hand in hand, enjoying their last night on the ship.

CHAPTER 18

Friday, April 23 – Washington, DC

They woke to find the ship docked back at Gravelly Point. Showered and dressed, they entered the dining room for a farewell breakfast. As always, the food and service were impeccable. Jon opted for poached eggs and corned beef hash served with a garnish of fresh fruit, and Kyle ordered a farmer's omelet filled with sausage, mushrooms, potatoes, and cheddar cheese.

Lingering over one last cup of coffee, they said goodbye to several of the waitstaff who had taken such good care of them for the previous four days.

"I guess we need to get going." Jon sounded sad.

"Yeah, but we still have a couple of days left before you head back to Arizona. Lots more memories to be made."

They retrieved their backpacks from their cabin and

disembarked, shaking hands with several of the crew on their way off the ship.

Before they knew it, they were back at Kyle's condo. Once inside, Jon kissed Kyle tenderly. "Thank you again for such a great vacation. I never expected a cruise on the Potomac, but it was wonderful."

"It really was," Kyle agreed. "But Sam gets much of the credit since she came up with the idea. Left to my own devices, I'd have just done a bunch of tourist stuff in the city. The cruise was much more romantic. I'll need to send Sam some flowers or something."

"That's a great idea, but let me do it. I'll send her something from both of us."

"Okay. Rob gave me the name of a florist in Westport that they use. I'll text you the name and number."

"Perfect."

They spent the day relaxing and just being together. They both seemed to crave time in each other's presence. After Kyle threw some clothes in the washer, they sat on the sofa leaning into each other and read.

Around one o'clock, Kyle stood up and stretched. "Interested in a bite to eat? I can make some pasta if you'd like."

"That sounds great."

They were just cleaning up from lunch when Kyle's phone buzzed. He turned to Jon as he wiped down the kitchen counter. "Uncle Mike made a reservation at Estadio for tonight at eight. It's an excellent tapas restaurant not too far from here. Is that okay with you?"

"It is. We had so much fun at the tapas place we went to in Albuquerque. It sounds great."

"Since we have several hours before we have to get ready, how would you feel about a little nap?"

Jon grinned slyly and grabbed Kyle's hand, leading him toward the stairs.

They fell into bed together, kissing each other gently. Then they napped ... eventually.

It was seven forty-five when Jon and Kyle arrived at Estadio. As Kyle approached the hostess station, he saw his aunt and uncle standing off to the side.

He hugged them both warmly. "You remember Jon."

"Of course," Ellen said. "How are you, Jon?"

"Fine, thank you," he replied, hugging Ellen and shaking Mike's hand. "I really appreciate you including me in dinner tonight. I told Kyle I'd be fine at his place, but he insisted I come along."

"Of course," Mike said. "After spending Christmas together, you're rather like family now, Jon."

Jon seemed to choke up a bit at Mike's words. "Thank you so much. That means a lot to me."

The hostess came over to tell them their table was ready.

Once seated, they quickly perused the drinks menu, and they all ordered the Spanish Old Fashioned.

"So, what brings you to DC, Jon?" Mike asked. "I was a bit surprised when Kyle said you were here this week."

Jon looked at Kyle, unsure of exactly what to say.

Jon's hand was resting on the table, and Kyle placed his hand over Jon's. "Jon's here because I invited him to come visit for the week. Actually, we're dating."

"Congrats!" Ellen's eyes shone. "When did this happen?"

"We spent a fair bit of time together when we were in England and got to know each other pretty well; we kept in contact once we got back," Kyle said. "Then I went out to Albuquerque in February to visit Jon while he was at a conference. I was pretty sure how I felt about Jon before he got here, and we just spent four days on a river cruise along the Potomac. We finally admitted our feelings for each other a couple of days ago."

Their waiter returned with drinks, and Mike raised his glass. "Here's to you guys; I hope you'll be very happy for many years to come."

"Thanks, Uncle Mike. That means a lot."

"I talked to your dad yesterday, Kyle, but he didn't say anything about Jon. Does he know?"

"I spoke to him and Rob a few weeks ago about it. He knows that Jon and I have been seeing each other, but I haven't spoken to him since we got off the ship this morning. I do plan on calling him tomorrow to share the news." Kyle sighed. "Frankly, he was a bit concerned because of the age difference, but I think Rob and I both made him realize that it wasn't as big a deal as he thought it was."

"Age is just a number," Ellen said. "If you really love each other, it won't be a problem."

"Okay, let's figure out what we want to eat," Mike said. "I'll order a bottle of Cava to celebrate. I want to officially welcome you to the family, Jon."

Dinner was wonderful. They shared a variety of small plates and chatted about a number of different topics, including the time they'd spent together in England a few months earlier.

As they lingered over espressos and churros, Mike turned to Jon. "So, Jon, have you ever thought about relocating to DC?"

Jon stared at him, shock clear on his face. "Well, um, I ..." he stammered. He sighed, head down for a moment. "Well, not really, but I have to admit, the thought did cross my mind in the last day or so."

"Really?" Kyle uttered. "You didn't say anything."

"Frankly, I'm still trying to process everything, but I am a little concerned about making a long-distance relationship work. While I was thinking about that, I did ponder living in DC for a moment or two." He glanced at Kyle, smiling. "It would make things easier for us, right?"

"It would," Kyle agreed. "But I figured we'd see how things went and talk about it eventually."

"Oh, of course," Jon continued. "I didn't mean to rush into things. It's just that when Mike mentioned moving here, my mouth kinda overtook my brain. No pressure, Kyle, really."

"Hey, it's fine, Jon. I was a little surprised but not in a bad way." Smiling, he looked at his uncle. "So, why did you bring this up, Uncle Mike?"

"Ahem ... well, first of all, sorry if I jumped the gun a bit. I know this is new for both of you, but I guess I just wanted Jon to keep in mind that if he does think about moving, to please let me know. Our practice is expanding, and we're always looking for capable paralegals to work for us."

Jon looked dumbfounded. "Seriously? You'd hire me?"

"No promises, but I have a good feeling about you, and

you are, after all, family. So yes, I'd do what I could for you, son."

"I have a bit of a situation at home with my mom, but Kyle came up with a possible solution, so once I can get that resolved, I'll be in touch." He paused, eyes wide, seeming to realize what he'd just said. "Um, I mean, once Kyle and I can discuss this and figure out what we want moving forward, I'll be in touch if I … I mean we … decide that me moving to DC is the right thing to do."

Kyle chuckled. "You're adorable when you're all nervous about saying the right thing, love. Relax. It's all good, and we'll figure this out."

───────────────

WHEN THEY GOT HOME, Jon kissed Kyle soundly, pushing him up against the door. "Wow, never in a million years did I expect your uncle to ask me about moving here. And also how they just took it all in stride about the two of us dating. This has been an amazing evening."

"Yeah, I knew they wouldn't have a problem with you and me. I mean, from what my dad said, Uncle Mike never had an issue with Dad's bisexuality. And even though I'd never actually come out one way or another before, I knew my family would be fine with whoever I dated."

"I'm a little jealous of that," Jon acknowledged. "Bernie has always been supportive of me. Hell, she probably knew I was gay before I did, but Mom's always been a challenge."

"Don't forget, you're part of my family now, so it's all good."

"I know. I'm a very lucky guy."

"So am I, love. So am I."

CHAPTER 19

Saturday, April 24 – Washington, DC

At the time Kyle and Jon were on their way home from the cruise, Kyle had gotten a text message from Neil. He'd left a bowl of fruit salad and a breakfast casserole in Kyle's fridge, with instructions on heating it up for brunch. Neil wanted to see Jon one more time before he flew back to Phoenix, but he also wanted to give Kyle and Jon some alone time, so he said he would be over for brunch around eleven. They could tell him all about their trip, then he'd get out of their hair.

As Kyle slipped the dish into the oven, he chuckled quietly. Neil was a great friend.

Why can't he meet the right guy? Ah well, that's a problem for another day.

He set a timer on his phone for ninety minutes, turned the

coffee maker on, and went back upstairs to wake Jon. They had time to work up a sweat before they showered.

AFTER CHATTING about the cruise over food and coffee—and several mimosas, thank you, Neil—they were sitting at the island when Neil got up to leave.

"I'm so very happy for the two of you," Neil said, hugging them both and kissing Jon on the cheek. "Safe travels home and I'll see you the next time you're in town."

"Thanks for everything, Neil," Jon replied. "I've got your number now, so don't be surprised if you get the occasional text."

Once he was gone, Kyle and Jon tidied up the kitchen, and Kyle said, "I'd like to call my dad and Rob." He grabbed his iPad and launched the FaceTime app.

"Hey, Dad," he said when Ben answered the call.

"Hi, guys." Ben turned away from the camera, "Sweetheart, it's Kyle and Jon." A moment later, Rob's face appeared on the screen next to Ben's. "Hey there. How was your cruise?"

"It was different but really good," Kyle said. He proceeded to briefly tell them about the trip and how it differed from a regular cruise.

"Sounds interesting," Ben commented. "We're glad you enjoyed yourselves. So, what else is going on?"

"Well," Kyle started, "we wanted to let you know that after spending even more time together, we realize that we love each other and want to do everything we can to make this work."

Ben's eyes shone brightly; he was clearly at a loss for words for a moment.

"That's wonderful," Rob said. "We're really happy for you both."

"Yes, we are," Ben finally said, his voice quivering a bit. "All I ever wanted was for you to be happy, son. And I'm sorry if I gave you the wrong impression when you first told me about Jon. Jon, you were already part of the family by way of Sam, but this solidifies it even more."

"Thanks, Ben, Rob. I'm thrilled to be part of this family. You're all really wonderful people."

"It's still a bit too early to know how things will work out," Kyle offered, "but there's a good chance that Jon will end up moving to DC. We had dinner with Uncle Mike and Aunt Ellen last night, and Uncle Mike talked to Jon about working at his firm."

"Wow, that's awesome," Rob said. "Please keep us posted on that."

"Will do. And how are you guys doing? How are the wedding plans coming along?"

Ben laughed, and Rob glared at him on the screen.

"Despite your father's amusement," Rob began, "things are going well." The start of a smile tugged at the corners of his mouth, and Kyle knew that Rob wasn't angry, just teasing his dad a bit.

Rob continued, "Save-the-date postcards will be going out to folks this coming week. As you know, we're getting married here at home in the backyard, and we're keeping it pretty small. But we wanted to give folks a heads-up since many of them will be invited to join us for the honeymoon celebration."

"Kyle was telling me about that," Jon interjected. "You're actually planning on taking people on your honeymoon with you?"

"Yeah, we really want this to be a celebration with those we love, so we decided to turn it all into a great big party. We're thinking about a Mediterranean cruise, but Sam also found a small island in the Caribbean that we could rent for a week, so that's a possibility too." Rob was visibly giddy with excitement as he explained. "And just this past week, she told me about another option, but I'm sworn to secrecy until she can get more details."

"The save-the-date card won't go into details about the trip yet, but we'll follow up in a month or so as soon as everything is decided," Ben added. "So Jon, if you do move to Washington and go to work for my brother, please make sure he understands that you'll need the time off. And even if you're still in Phoenix, you'll need to take a vacation in October."

"Okay, I will. Thanks."

"Well, it sounds like you've got everything under control, Rob. You too, Dad. Please let me know if I can do anything to help out. For now, we'll say goodbye, but I'll talk to you soon. Love you, guys."

"Love you too, son. And love you, Jon. Again, welcome to the family."

"Love you both," Rob added before they ended the call.

"I'm so glad they found each other." Kyle looked at Jon. "I've never seen my dad happier. Now, how about we go for a little walk in the neighborhood? If you end up moving here, you'll need to get familiar with where everything is."

CHAPTER 20

Sunday, April 25 – Washington, DC

Kyle stared at the top of Jon's head and smiled. Jon was leaving that afternoon, and he knew he'd miss this.

They snuggled close—Jon's head lay on Kyle's chest, and his arm reached across Kyle's belly. Kyle's arm draped down Jon's back, his hand resting on the swell of Jon's ass. He didn't want the moment to end.

He thought back to his flight home from England at the end of the past year. He remembered thinking that all good things come to an end, but that hadn't happened, had it? Thankfully, he and Jon had kept in touch, and everything had changed in ways he had never imagined.

Jon stirred slightly, and Kyle pulled him closer.

Kyle was having trouble sorting out his feelings. On the

one hand, he was thrilled things were going well between him and Jon. He'd never felt that strongly about someone before, and it felt good. Right.

But part of him was nervous. There was a tension that puzzled him. He knew he loved Jon and that Jon loved him. So, what was causing those other feelings? Maybe it was just that they had a lot to get through. What if things didn't work out with switching homes with Bernie? What if Jon's mom hated Kyle when they finally met? What if things fell apart, and Jon couldn't or wouldn't move to DC?

Stop it, he told himself. *Stop overthinking this!*

Jon sighed and gazed up at him. "I can almost see the wheels turning in that head of yours, Kyle. What's wrong?"

"Nothing, really." Kyle sighed. "Just letting my brain run rampant. Overthinking everything. You know, the usual." He chuckled lightly.

"Hey, babe, it's gonna be okay." Jon slid upward and pecked him lightly on the lips. "It may take a while, but we *will* make this work."

"I know. It's just that sometimes my head doesn't listen to my heart." He smiled at Jon. "As much as I'd love to spend at least part of the day in bed with you, we should get up. What do you want for breakfast?"

"You." Jon laughed, tickling Kyle's sides, kissing his neck.

Okay, maybe they could spend a few more minutes in bed.

<hr>

KYLE WAS WALKING BACK to his condo from the Metro station. He'd dropped Jon off at the airport and dreaded going back to an empty home. He couldn't put it off forever, but he could delay it a bit. He stopped at a little store on the way and picked up a few things: yogurt, some strawberries, a loaf of whole-grain bread, a head of broccoli, and a few other things he needed.

As he reached the door of his condo, his phone rang. Pulling it out of his pocket, he saw's Neil's photo on the screen, so he answered.

"Hey, Neil, what's going on?"

"I figured you were sitting at home wallowing in the loss of your man, so I thought I'd call and cheer you up, of course."

"Aw, thanks. I'm just Ig home. Stopped to pick up a few things on my way back from the airport. Hang on a sec."

He put the bag down on the counter.

"Do you want to come Iver? I can thaw out some chicken and fix dinner for us if you'd like." He hoped Neil said yes; he really didn't want to be alone.

"Sure. Give me an hour or so, and I'll head over. I'll bring wine."

"Great. That will give me some time to start some laundry. See you soon." *Good ol' Neil, he knew just what I needed.*

He put his groceries away and was getting his dirty clothes from the clothes hamper when his phone buzzed again:

> Just boarding now. Miss U already. xoxo

So he answered:

> Miss U 2. Neil's coming over 4 dinner. Will call U 2morrow. Love U

Everything was going to work out, he just knew it.

EPILOGUE

July

The summer was flying by.

Jon had approached Bernie and Jeff with Kyle's idea about them switching houses, and after discussing a few details, they were all for it. Jon's house was larger, and with the kids getting older, they could use the extra room. Bernie also agreed that since their mom would spend more time with her existing grandchildren, it might help take the pressure off Jon to start a family.

When they finally sat down with their mom, she wasn't as resistant to it as they had feared, so they quickly moved forward to make it all happen before she changed her mind. Between a friend of Jeff's who worked in real estate and a lawyer friend of Jon's, they got all the paperwork drawn up and signed.

During all of that, Kyle visited Jon in Phoenix a couple of times, and Louisa actually liked him, which was more than Jon could say about his past boyfriends. Things were definitely working out.

At one point, Jon was discussing plans with Bernie regarding switching houses. "When do you think you'll be ready to make the move, sis?"

"We've started packing things up, and I'd like to get it done before the kids start school again. Granted, they're not switching schools or anything, but it will just be easier on them to get it done sooner, I think. Is that gonna work for you?"

"Yeah, I can do whatever works for you," Jon said. "In fact, there's something I've been meaning to tell you."

"Oh? I've gotta be honest," Bernie said. "You've seemed a bit distracted lately. Everything is okay with you and Kyle, right?"

"Yeah, it is. In fact, that's kind of what I wanted to talk to you about." He took a deep breath and pushed forward. "If things work out the way I think they will, I'm probably gonna be moving to DC, sis."

"Ha! I knew it!" Bernadette exclaimed. "I told Jeff I thought that might happen. You're not even gonna move into our house, are you?"

"My original plan was to relocate to your house, but now, depending on the whole move schedule, I may be there for a little while, but I'll end up storing most of my stuff rather than moving it to the house. I really won't need any of it in Washington, since I'll be living with Kyle. I figure I can just rent out the house here for the time being. If things work out with Kyle long-term, I can always sell it later."

Pausing, he took a breath and said, "So you're not upset with me?"

"Of course not, sweetie. When I saw how serious you and Kyle were getting, I figured it was only a matter of time. But what about work?"

"Kyle's uncle is a family lawyer in DC, and he mentioned that they were expanding and suggested I might want to apply there. In fact, I'm flying out to see Kyle in a little over a week and will have an in-person interview while I'm there."

"They'd be stupid not to hire you." Jon smiled at her vote of confidence.

"Thanks, Bernie. I appreciate your faith in me. Okay, not to change the subject, but I've got to get my ass in gear. Let me know when you have a firmer move date, and I'll make arrangements to store most of this stuff. Love you."

"Love you too, Jon."

---

*S*EPTEMBER

JON SAT AT THE GATE, waiting for his flight. He couldn't believe everything had worked out. After one in-person interview and three video calls, he had been offered a job at Mike's firm. That's when things had really gotten crazy.

One condition he had requested when interviewing was that he'd need some time off in October for a very important wedding that he couldn't miss. Since Mike was also taking time off for Ben and Rob's nuptials, he understood the request and helped make that happen. But that meant that the firm wanted Jon to start work in September so that he could get settled in his new position before leaving for vacation.

August had become a whirlwind of activity: packing up most of his home and putting everything but his bed and a few personal things into storage, moving said bed to Bernie's old house, and shipping most of his clothes and some books and such to Kyle's condo.

And spending time with his best friend, Teresa. T was saddened by his decision to move, but she completely understood and continued to support him in every way that she could. She'd met Kyle when he visited Jon and confirmed that he was a catch and that she'd move to be with him too. In fact, she was already talking about visiting Jon and Kyle in DC, so Jon concluded that T was in his life to stay.

Jon's phone buzzed:

> Can't wait to see you, sweetheart. I'll be waiting for you at the airport.

Jon smiled, sending a kiss emoji and a heart in response.

A year ago, he had never imagined that he'd meet the man of his dreams and move across the country. Who could have known that he'd do just that and find love on the Potomac?

The End

A LETTER FROM RJ

Dear Reader,

Thank you so much for reading Love on the Potomac. The next book in this series is Love in the Mediterranean. Rob and Ben are getting married! Neil is surprised to receive an invitation to the wedding, but Kyle convinces him to attend not only the ceremony but also the honeymoon party on a Mediterranean cruise, where Neil meets the man of his dreams and finds true love.

Be sure to follow me on Amazon to be notified of new releases, and look for me on Facebook for sneak peeks of upcoming stories.

Please take a moment to write a review of Love on the Potomac on Amazon and Goodreads. Reviews can make all the difference in helping a book show up in Amazon searches.

To to sign up for my newsletter, stop by rj-peterson.ck.page.

We have a great reader group on Facebook that can be found here: www.facebook.com/groups/rjpetersonsadventurers/

Finally, several of my titles are available on audio, narrated by the amazing Kevin Earlywine or the fabulous Cole Kurtz. They can be found here: link.rjpeterson.net/audio

Happy reading!

RJ

P.S. Keep going for a free download!

FREE SHORT STORY

Download a copy of His Elevator Pitch

Inspired by a writing prompt, His Elevator Pitch is the story of River, an unemployed executive assistant, and Thom, the department head of a prestigious multi-faceted corporation.

When a power failure takes out several city blocks in Boston, MA, they find themselves stuck in an elevator with nothing but time on their hands.

Conversation ensues and when power is restored, River goes off to his interview, thinking that's the end of his encounter with the handsome stranger. Or is it?

This story features many of the themes my writing is known for: older guys, sweet-with-heat encounters, low or no angst, and always a happily ever after.

SCAN THE CODE TO DOWNLOAD

About the Author

Hi, I'm RJ! I'm a retired graphic designer. An avid reader—preferably while sipping a vodka martini or bourbon on the rocks—I've had a long and varied career, including library page, car wash attendant, travel agent, and graphic designer in the marijuana industry. In addition, I worked in the banking industry for twenty-five years. I love to travel and have been on 60+ cruises. When not on a cruise, my husband & I live in New England.

I never planned to be a writer, but a fateful day in January, 2021 changed it all. I woke with a story stuck in my head and started typing. The more I type, the more story ideas I get.

Find all my links here:

WANT TO READ MORE?

The New Adventures in Love Series:

Love On The Horizon

Love For The Holidays

Love On The Potomac

Love In The Mediterranean

Love Is For Family

(Coming in 2025)

Hawthorne Bluff Series:

Finding Finlay

Addicted to Ashton

Chasing Courtland

(Coming in 2026)

SEAsons of Love Series:

Love at Frost Sight

Resting Grinch Face

Don't Claus a Scene

Great Chemis-Tree

Stand Alone Stories

The Locket's Tale

Footprints on My Heart

(Coming in 2025)

All my book links in one place!